Curses and Faith

Whitney Hill

Benu Media
6409 Fayetteville Rd
Ste 120 #155
Durham, NC 27713
(984) 244-0250
benumedia.com

To receive special offers, release updates, and bonus content, sign up for our newsletter: go.benumedia.com/newsletter

ISBN (ebook): 978-1-7376311-3-2
ISBN (pbook): 978-1-7376311-4-9

Library of Congress Control Number: 2021924127

Cover Designer: Pintado (99Designs)
Editor: Jeni Chappelle (Jeni Chappelle Editorial)

Content Warnings

This book contains consensual on-page sex, physical violence, gore, non-fatal car accidents, blood-drinking, on-page death, swearing, slurs (not toward any real racial or ethnic group/identity), alcohol use, knife violence, threat of sexual violence, and a scene where a character is unable to breathe.

It's also a steamy vampire romance with a happy ending, so make sure you have something to cool down with afterward!

Chapter 1: Lya

I sat on the beach watching the tide come in as the sun set, chucking shells into the crashing waves as I wrestled with my thoughts. The whole two-wolves meme, only instead of wolves I had a happy life with my vampire lover on one side and a burdensome debt to the head bitch of the Carolinas on the other.

The last three months had been good. Real bloody good, no pun intended. Enough that I finally trusted Cade would be there for me, unlike the family and ex-boyfriend who'd stood by while I was tried and then exiled. Shit had hit the fan in North Carolina, and instead of leaving me to deal with the fallout, Cade had been at my side. Our cozy love shack in St. Augustine was his and I lived there rent-free, other than a monthly blood donation I was happy to give.

Five hundred miles, an eight-hour drive, and all the love in the world didn't mean shit against my debts in North Carolina though.

The surf kissed my toes as I wrestled with how to respond to the text message I'd gotten while we'd slept this afternoon: *Time to pay off what you owe.*

Nothing else. No details, no targets. Nothing for a twice-exiled, half-elven bounty hunter like me to make a plan with. Just the vague threat that the favor I owed in exchange for the new life I'd been living was due. Knowing Callista, it was something that meant my blissful contentment was about to shatter.

She didn't do gentle, easy, or reasonable. She did whatever the fuck she wanted and hang everyone around her—regardless of what her demands cost them.

It'd worked in my favor for the months I'd served my exile in the Triangle as a bail bond runner and occasional supernatural bounty hunter. It'd worked a little more when it meant she could afford to flip the middle finger to the Lyon and Chapel Hill Conclaves and get me the hell out of her territory. But I'd pissed her off in doing so and, possibly more damning, had agreed to owe her a favor in exchange for leaving town with my life and Cade's. I suspected there wasn't anywhere in the world, on this plane or any of the others I couldn't reach anyway, that someone could go to escape Callista calling in a debt.

As the sun kissed the horizon, I rose and trudged back to the car, making the short drive home to Cade's haven just outside the Historic District. Live oaks and palmettos hugged the gravel path that served as a driveway, completely overgrown by design behind the tall fence. Living as a vampire and a half-elf amidst humans required more than a little privacy, and the thick foliage helped block the sun. The house was old, and we'd had to upgrade the wiring for electricity, even if we didn't use it much. Most of that usage was me, looking for and securing work in the small local Otherside community so I wouldn't feel completely reliant on the wealth Cade had established in his nearly five hundred years on Earth.

Yeah, I deserved to be looked after. Didn't mean I was foolish enough not to establish my own source of income. I'd had to leave Lyon suddenly and Durham after that. I wasn't about to get cute with my financial security now. And as much as I loved and trusted Cade, I'd been burned before. It left me anxious sometimes. Maintaining an identity apart from being a vampire's girlfriend helped.

I did love him. I just needed my space. A lot of it.

I waved off some hungry mosquitoes and pushed open the door to the screened lanai then the next one into the house proper. Everything was quiet and still. As a half-elf, my crepuscular schedule had overlapping hours with Cade's, but I was more likely to be active at dusk and dawn, when he was winding up and settling down. It was the new moon, which meant I was more awake and he was more heavily asleep.

Perfect for taking my mind off Callista.

He was still crashed out in the bed we shared during the day when I made my way back to the bedroom. I leaned against the doorframe, unable to help my smile as I studied him.

Almost two meters of unfairly sexy vampire sprawled among black silk sheets, his pale skin a contrast and his dark brown hair almost lost against the pillows, eyes the same shade hidden behind closed lids. He'd rolled to my side of the bed again, as he did sometimes when I got up before him, and his hand stretched to the now-empty space where I'd been.

Time to do something about that.

I stripped the beach wrap and bikini I'd donned and stalked back to the bed. Stealthy as I was, he woke with the sharp, unnatural inhale that said he'd registered a threat. I dodged the first defensive swipe and the second but was caught by the third and unable to help my laugh as he pinned me, arms overhead and teeth at my throat. I held very still then, heart pounding in an equal blend of anticipation and healthy fear. He inhaled, taking the scent from the corner of my jaw to my collarbone.

"Lya." Cade pulled back and frowned at me, lips tight even as his hips ground against me.

"Hey babe." I wiggled, just to make him grip my wrists harder.

"One of these days—"

"One of these days nothing. We're a long way away from the last time."

The last time being the time back in North Carolina when he'd nearly drained me while more than halfway to his second death, after I'd already consented.

"If I hurt you…"

I shook my head. "You won't, or I wouldn't be here."

He caressed my neck then glanced at the curtained window, seeking the answer to a question he hadn't asked. "New moon."

"Mm-hm."

He didn't press me. He never did. My blood was mine to offer, not his to coerce, beg, cajole, or hint after. But all at once, his attention sharpened, and he was a hungry vampire with a half-elf pinned beneath him—a valuable source of more powerful blood than he'd typically be able to get willingly or without incident.

He could take my blood. Kill me, even. But he wouldn't, a fact I trusted completely because of everything we'd already been through.

If only it was that easy to free myself from the ghosts between us, keeping me from the deeper commitment I suspected Cade craved.

For tonight though, things were simple. I knew what he wanted. What he hoped for. It was mine to offer or deny, and I loved the power I held over a centuries-old vampire. "Thirsty?"

He swallowed, and the caress was briefly a squeeze around my throat as he shuddered. "Yes. For you, always."

A thrill ran through me at the edge of a growl in his voice. I let him drink from me every new moon, when my power crested and his was at its lowest ebb. We'd learned I didn't need the full six weeks a human would to recover from a blood donation, and he'd gotten much more enthusiastic about it when I'd confessed that I liked being glamoured.

I pulled him down to kiss me then whispered, "Drink."

I didn't need to tell him to make me feel good after. He did that instinctively, as much from his own nature as from having drunk from me enough times to have a few physiological responses kick in that ensured he preserved my good graces.

Cade didn't need to be told twice. He gripped my chin to tilt my head, and I locked eyes with him. The whites of his eyes were lost to black as his pupils expanded and his magic was freed. Vampire glamour slithered over me, drowning me in a swirling mental euphoria. Not a full glamour but enough. His thumb dragged over the skin of my throat as I slumped. Physical ecstasy joined the experience as he sank his teeth into my neck and his magic transmuted the pain of his bite to pure pleasure.

I gasped, my body arching up against his until the paralytic effect kicked in. He gathered me close and drank deeper. Each swallow seemed to go straight to his groin as his cock hardened.

After a few more swallows, he pressed his tongue against the bite, healing it as much as he could before pulling away. "Lya?"

I groaned, the best I could manage as I floated in the depths of the glamour.

"You know the drill. Say it."

"I want you," I managed. "Please."

He'd said I'd beg him for this, and he was right. We'd gone over it carefully before trying this the first time, discussing impacts and consent, and I'd started craving it. The swirling embrace of glamour, the sharp pain-pleasure of his bite, the satisfaction of the fuck that followed.

He didn't go straight for it, taking his time with my body and giving me time to come out of the paralyzing effect of the glamour a little in case I changed my mind. I never did, but he was even bigger on enthusiastic consent than most vampires, given how his sire and master had abused him.

His tongue was busy between my thighs when I found enough sense to say, "Please, Cade. More."

Then my arms were pinned overhead, and the earlier bliss joined new ecstasy as every stroke of him into me hit something sensitive and pleasurable. The paralytic effect wore off completely, and the more I fought him, the tighter he held me and the faster he moved against me, striving to claim me before I could break free.

My climax hit me hard. I held him in place with my calves against his ass as I pushed up against him, grinding my hips to take my own pleasure. When I shuddered and relaxed he took his turn, drawing me into a second climax as he reached his.

As always, he shifted me into a recovery position after he withdrew: laying on my side, head tilted up slightly to ensure a clear airway. Again, instinctive rather than strictly necessary, but I was still mostly adrift in glamour and sex. I liked that he cared enough to make sure I was okay.

He curled up against my back and buried his nose against the nape of my neck. "Are you well?"

I groaned, feeling far better than okay.

"Verbal, love."

"Yes."

He kissed my throat. "You'll need a scarf again."

I did my best to shrug, not caring in the slightest about scarves to cover hickeys and half-healed bite marks in the Florida heat when I could feel this good. Hell, I'd forgotten about Callista and my guilt-ridden doubts for at least half an hour.

"Lya?"

"I'm fine," I mumbled, annoyed with myself for the hint of discord and tension that thinking of Callista had brought to an otherwise perfect new moon. "Just hold me."

He obliged, tucking closer and tracing a finger lightly over the partly healed punctures in my neck. "Even better than last time."

I tried to reply, "Good," but slipped into a dreamless sleep before the word left my lips.

***

The next time I woke it was full dark. Cade's warmth and the woodsmoke, iron, and granite scent of him enveloped me.

"Hey," I said.

He startled. Probably dozing, unlikely as it seemed with a couple fresh pints of Othersider blood in him. "Are you okay?"

"Hungry." I'd learned to be honest after our first romp after arriving here. It got us both what we needed—me some food and him the sense that he wasn't a beast boosting his own lifespan by drinking from his girlfriend.

Which he was. It was mutually agreed-upon, but Cade was funny about it sometimes. Fair play given my own hang-ups, which probably weren't helping him feel better about it.

We were trying. We had time.

He lightly kissed the spot where he'd bitten me before sliding out of bed and heading for the kitchen. As the clatter of pots and pans signaled he was getting some breakfast in order, I took a minute to stretch both my body and my Aetheric senses. My weak wards hadn't registered anything other than the usual raccoons, possums, tortoises, rabbits, and birds, so I took my time getting out of bed. There'd be time enough to fret and rush when Callista got around to telling me what she actually wanted.

Cade looked up when I emerged from the bedroom, his eyebrows lifting and the corner of his mouth curling up in appreciation as he took in my choice of dress: the loose cotton swim cover-up and nothing else.

"That looks like an invitation," he said, his voice pitched low and easy and his motions smooth as he turned the bacon.

I smiled. "I'm going back out for a swim later."

The beaches were closed after sunset, but it wasn't like a mundane could stop me.

The look he gave me said clearer than words that I'd be doing nothing of the sort if he had any say in it, but he didn't get weird and over-possessive like other vamps—one of the reasons I didn't give in to my reflex to flee anything resembling this level of intimacy. He just turned back to the new stove we'd had installed. Cade had never needed to cook here, but I, for better or worse, was mortal and wanted to eat hot meals in my escape from all the shit I'd been dragging with me since I'd been exiled from Lyon and lost my bounty hunting work in London in one terrible blow. This had been a chance to take a break and figure out who I was in this new life, with no pressure…until now.

My stomach clenched again, and Cade frowned at whatever that did to my scent. From his expression, he was trying to parse the different layers. This was hunger, that was blood loss, and underneath was fear. All he did was plate the food though, knowing I had a bad habit of running if confronted any way other than physically.

"Thanks," I said, as much for the food as for his patience.

He leaned over to kiss the top of my head before snagging a Gatorade for me from the fridge we'd gotten at the same time as the stove.

I'd just started tucking in when my phone chirped. We both recognized the tone signaling it was Callista. The flavorful bacon and eggs suddenly tasted like ash my mouth, but I still shoveled another forkful in.

Cade frowned. "Don't tell me you already know what Callista wants."

"I know what she wants. I'm ignoring her." I stabbed at the eggs.

"Lya—"

"I know I owe her. She doesn't have Watchers in St. Augustine, and it is entirely legitimate that I'm just now waking up."

He subsided, glowering.

"I'll deal with it." The weight of his eyes in the low light made me hunch. I had a tendency to run away from my problems, and I was afraid he was slowly getting tired of it. This debt wasn't the kind of thing one could run from though. "I said I'll deal with it, okay? I just want to have a good new moon."

What neither of us said was that if Callista was calling in her debt, it might be our last one for a while.

Chapter 2: Lya

Late morning brought a completely separate set of problems.

I was drifting in the stubbornly half-asleep way I did when I was trying to ignore a problem that wouldn't go away—in this case, debating what to say to Callista's follow-up text that she'd be collecting her debt in the form of a task, still no details. I think she was just trying to draw out the anxiety of it, the bitch.

Cade was curled up as close to me as he could get, one arm across my chest, his face buried against the curve of my neck and shoulder. I wouldn't have taken a centuries-old pirate-turned-supernatural-predator for an affectionate, overgrown cat, but it was one of life's better surprises.

Then again, maybe cat wasn't quite it. Yeah, it was cute, but it was also quite literally hanging on to blood he'd claimed and ensuring I carried his scent. I chose to accept it for what it was intended to be—affection and protectiveness, not control. I liked the protectiveness. I liked that he wanted me. It was reassuring.

At the edge of my awareness, one of the Aetheric wards I'd set around the property twanged. Something big. Not a deer. Bipedal. I tried to slide out of bed without waking Cade, but between drinking my blood last night and his own protective instincts, the sun didn't have him completely under its sway.

"Ly?" he said.

I leaned back to whisper in his ear. "Shh. Someone's crossed the property line."

He came fully awake, pressing up to sniff and shaking his head when the closer scents—us, sex, food, the usual—covered up anyone farther out. He knew as well as I did that if anyone was coming here, they were either completely ignorant of the fact that it was a vampire's lair or they knew and didn't mean Cade well since they hadn't announced themselves in advance, as was proper between Othersiders. He might be the more dangerous of the two of us, but I had the advantage of being unknown and unaffected by sunlight. I could handle myself if it was door number two.

I brushed a kiss on his cheek and pulled on yesterday's shorts and T-shirt as quickly and quietly as I could. I grabbed the Sawback machete alongside the back door and slunk out, which would let me circle round behind the intruder, moving as quietly as I could in the dry underbrush of our yard.

They continued to approach slowly, too stealthy to be human. From the way my magic wrapped them, they were…a wereanimal?

Something was off about that though. I didn't like it.

I approached downwind and spotted a small man creeping through the palmettos, eyes fixed on the house. He was dark-haired as Cade but with lighter eyes, tan in the way pale-skinned people were tan, like someone who'd lived in the Florida sun a long time. My nose wasn't as good as Cade's or a full-blooded elf, but even to me he carried musky scents—plural, not just wolf or cat or bear. All of them, somehow. I frowned.

That shouldn't be possible. Weres rarely mixed species and even more rarely interbred. It was theoretically possible for an individual to have more than one shape, but something about the way my skin crawled told me this was no were, regardless of what he smelled like.

Fuck this. I eased closer and was rewarded with a startled jump when I tapped his shoulder with my machete before hovering it alongside his neck.

"Stop moving," I said.

Whoever he was, he was smart enough to listen and raise his hands. "And who might you be?"

"You're not in a position to ask any questions, given that you're trespassing."

He turned his head slightly, offering me a mischievous grin over his shoulder. "Am I?"

"You sure as shit weren't invited. Now shut up and keep walking but quit hiding."

The grin flickered into a twist of resentful outrage before resuming as he started walking again. "As you wish."

Cade was waiting in the shade of the north-facing front porch as we walked up. He narrowed his eyes, and his lip twitched into the beginnings of a snarl before he forced himself to neutrality. "Alejandro."

My captive inclined his head in the old-timey way I'd seen in a few movies. "Cade. It's been a while."

I accidentally-on-purpose tapped this Alejandro's neck with the flat of the machete. "If you two know each other, you want to explain why you didn't announce yourself?"

Alejandro just grinned again. I was really starting not to like him.

"He's a turnskin who's helped me as many times as he's stabbed me in the back," Cade said flatly.

I frowned and gave a half-shake of my head, not familiar with the phrase "turnskin."

"He's a blood witch who's stolen animal and wereanimal bone or skin and uses them to shapeshift himself." Disgust was clear in Cade's tone.

It was all I could do not to recoil. That was utterly disgusting and reprehensible. I looked at the thongs of leather around his neck with new understanding.

"You say stolen," Alejandro said. "I say took a bounty."

Bile splashed in my throat. I'd taken plenty of bounties. I never dismembered them to keep pieces.

Alejandro glanced at me again. "Who's this one? She wouldn't give me her name."

"Then she's smarter than I was," Cade snapped. "What do you want?"

"Call off your woman and let's have a conversation. Like friends, hm?"

Cade wrestled with that, probably equally for wondering what the hell this turnskin would dare a vampire's lair to talk about as much as for knowing the futility of telling me to do anything. "No, I don't think I will. You approached in daylight. This isn't a friendly visit."

"Maybe I was just testing you, old friend. I've heard rumors, you know."

Cade's gaze flicked to me. Something about these rumors bothered him or presented a danger. I stiffened, wanting this man gone even if it meant a fight, but this was Cade's land and Cade's acquaintance. I wasn't going to play the fool though. In a breath, I drew on Aether and laid a light tracking tag on Alejandro. If he fucked with us, I'd know where to go for payback. When it settled, I lifted the machete away.

"Good wench," Alejandro said.

I smacked him good in the temple with the flat of the blade, and he spun around to glare at me.

I smiled. "Oops."

"Alejandro," Cade called in a low, sharp tone as the witch kept glaring. "She's mine."

That sounded possessive, but it felt good. Cade would have my back when I needed him. I wasn't just a meal or a fuck to him.

With a last narrowing of his eyes, our rude guest inclined his head to me just enough to be acceptable.

I smirked right back at him, unwilling to give an inch.

"We'll treat on the porch." Cade disappeared back inside.

I followed Alejandro up the stairs and into the lanai, giving him enough space that, if he decided to try something, I'd have breathing room to wield the Sawback.

Alejandro made himself at home in one of the weather-beaten wooden chairs on the low porch, looking around like he'd been here before. "Love what you've done with the place."

I didn't reply, leaning with my back against the wall of the house as I reached with Aether to see if there was anyone else out there and reset the ward he'd tripped at the fence line.

"I can see why he likes you. Attractive, just dangerous enough to be worth playing with, and—"

"Leave off, Alejandro." Cade re-emerged with a glass of water and a packet of jerky. As he handed both to the witch, he offered the standard Otherside greeting between people who weren't going to kill each other just yet. "Be welcome in my home. My table is yours, my hearth is yours, and my roof is yours, while you are here." The little growl in his tone said he didn't quite mean it, but the formality was necessary regardless.

Alejandro accepted the food and drink. "I honor my hosts. While your home is mine, my strength is yours."

When he'd had a bite of meat and a sip of water, Cade sat in the chair deepest in the porch's shadows. "Talk."

"Early for you to be up. Or late."

"You risked me draining you to observe my sleeping habits?"

"I risked you draining me to see if it was really you." Alejandro's gaze darted to me then back to Cade. "Morris came to see me, a year or so ago now."

My fist tightened involuntarily on my blade. Cade's abusive sire and master had been a real piece of work in the worst way.

Alejandro smirked. "She met him?"

"I killed him," I snapped. At the turnskin's considering glance, I shut my mouth. This was Cade's gig.

"What did Morris want?" Cade asked coolly.

"The usual. To kill you, slowly and painfully. Gods but he was a bore."

"The usual? He visited more than once?"

"You really thought you'd killed him, didn't you." Alejandro shook his head. "Idiot. I hope she made a better job of it than you did because that fucker had what was coming to him." Smoldering rage flickered, chased by a hint of respect as he looked at me again. "You really ended him?"

I glanced at Cade, who nodded. "Shot him six times with silver," I said, "including once in the brain, and then beheaded him."

"Oh, I like her." Alejandro's earlier impish antagonism flipped to delighted malice. "I'm almost sorry for not coming properly. It'd be better for all of us if we trusted each other."

"Why's that?" Cade asked. "Given that the last time I trusted you, you stuck silver in my back."

I ground my teeth to stop myself from asking why exactly it was that we'd invited this trickster incarnate to our home and given him guest right.

"Because Morris was paying for information about you in gold," Alejandro said.

That meant something to Cade because his face blanked. "Not—"

"Yes. And when I told him to fuck himself after he'd spent everything from the cache here, he laughed and said he had more. Including something so valuable that even that infernal bitch Callista would be interested."

Pieces shifted in my brain, and suddenly, I had a bloody good idea what Callista's job might be. This had to be why she'd sidelined Torsten to post a bounty on Cade, a legal vagabond, and why she'd been willing to let us go in exchange for a favor. She knew whatever this treasure was—because if they were talking gold, it had to be a treasure—that she'd just need to bide her time before something about it came to light. Then she could leverage me to be her good little hound to fetch it for her. Damn her.

Cade leaned back in his chair, steepled his fingers, and sank into the stillness only the undead could manage.

It was a little less still than usual though, enough that Alejandro frowned and glanced between us. His eyes landed on the twin dimples on my neck. "Ah. That's how you're up. The half-elf is your pet?"

I couldn't help stiffening. I'd assumed I was Cade's girlfriend, but we'd never put a label on it and vampires were far more likely to have pets. Was that all I was? A valuable pet? Had I misread the situation?

"All you need to know is that she's mine." Cade leveled a warning look at him. "And if you so much as look at her in a way she doesn't like, I'll carry out my previous threat."

Alejandro snorted. "In a way *she* doesn't like. Whipped."

Cade moved so fast that neither Alejandro nor I caught it. The scent of the witch's fear flooded the porch even as all the fungi and ferns in a three-meter radius burst up and grew at least a few centimeters.

Cade's grip closed around the witch's throat. "Don't make me rescind guest right to *my* house and let her do what I know she's thinking of, given how she's holding that machete right now. I do love to watch her work."

This was why I loved the man. Yeah, he was the bigger threat. But he let me take care of my own problems.

Alejandro looked like he had something more to say about that, but he swallowed hard against Cade's palm and slowly extended his hands. "My apologies, miss. It's been a while since my manners mattered, and I seem to have forgotten them."

"If you find them quick and tell us what the hell you want, I might forgive you." I let a toothy grin spread across my face that said clear as day I wouldn't forget. I didn't know what kind of history Cade had with this guy, but it seemed like the treacherous kind and I wasn't keen on getting myself killed.

"I'd be obliged." Alejandro looked at Cade then, and something passed between them as the witch raised his eyebrows. "No blood, no foul?"

Cade backed off with poor grace, sinking back into his chair. "You have ten seconds to get to the point of your visit. Including why you came in daylight if you truly thought I was the only one here."

Alejandro shrugged. "There aren't many Othersiders in town, but I heard from a trickster hare that an old blood drinker and a new dusk walker were in town. You're the only vagabond who's ever stopped here long enough for one of them to notice. Most of the rest of your kind pass through to Miami. Wasn't hard to guess you were here. But you'd only come if you were looking for something or running from something else. I'm willing to bet I guessed right on which." He grinned maliciously. "I just wanted to get the drop on you to make a point."

Of course he was aligned with the tricksters.

But what would Cade be looking for? He hadn't said anything when we'd decided to come down here, nor had he made any effort to look for anything as far as I'd noticed. I kept my face blank and bored, as though I knew exactly what was going on, but my earlier doubts about what I was to Cade grew. I shoved them down. Now wasn't the time.

"One of these days your points are going to get you killed, and I almost hope I'm there for it," Cade said after a quick glance at me. "Fine. So Morris spent one treasure and hinted at another. He's dead, and I'm the only one left who knows where his other caches are. You want me to tell you, in exchange for…"

"Helping you secure it. Morris was too badly hurt to be discreet, so you might want to avoid Miami unless you want to play with Santiago and Luz." He spread his hands. "I'm not the only one who knows, just the only one who knows where to find *you*. And knows of your connection to Morris, of course."

How old was this turnskin?

As though he could hear my thought, he glanced at me, and his lips curled up in a smile. "Your…lady…would be an excellent addition to the expedition, as long as she keeps her weapons away from my head."

"No promises," I said with a smile as sharp as one of Cade's, despite my lacking fangs.

Cade sat quiet for a minute, studying me before turning back to Alejandro. "Come back tomorrow. Sunset. I'll have an answer for you then."

The men shook hands. I pointedly kept mine to myself, and Alejandro was smart enough not to push before swinging the lanai door open and stepping off the porch in one long step. He whistled as he walked away.

When I moved to follow, Cade said, "Don't bother. He played his trick and got caught. He'll be honest until tomorrow night."

"If you say so."

Rubbing his eyes tiredly, Cade rose and extended a hand.

I stared at him, lips pressed tight. Now that Alejandro didn't need to be the focus of my bad mood, Cade was going to get his share of it.

He sighed. "I'll explain everything inside. I just need to get out of the daylight."

"Fine." Something in me wanted to keep him out here, to punish him for whatever the fuck this had been, but I reminded myself he didn't owe me all his secrets. In five centuries, he'd have picked up so many that he'd probably forgotten some.

Not this one though, this sounded big.

As he stripped in the bedroom, I threw myself in the room's lone armchair and hugged my knees to my chest. The chair was threadbare and a little musty from all the humidity, but I wasn't ready to go back to bed just yet. I didn't even want to be seated but if I didn't anchor myself I'd be out the door, fleeing the ghosts of my past for at least a few hours. I needed to face this. "So you proposed Florida because there was a treasure here?"

"Mainly for the property but yes." Cade threw himself back on the bed, belly down. "I was hoping we could claim the treasure. But I didn't want to get your hopes up. Given what Alejandro said, I was right not to."

I relaxed a little. That was fair and lined up with what I knew of him. But it still irked me that he hadn't told me. I'd already been burned once by someone I thought loved me. I wanted this time to be different, but this made it hard.

I shook it off. Trust. I needed to trust him. "So one treasure's gone, but there's another one."

Cade looked at me, his dark eyes giving nothing away. "Multiple others, but yes. One in particular in North Carolina. The Outer Banks."

So I'd been right. Callista must have spent the last few months plotting.

Now she was ready to have me do her dirty work.

Chapter 3: Cade

Of all the people from Cade's past for Lya to meet, it had to be Alejandro. One of the least trustworthy in a crowd of murderous miscreants and therefore one of the most likely to fuck Cade's efforts to get her to settle down and stop looking over her shoulder all the time.

And of course, the first thing he'd brought up was the fucking treasure. Which, from the new suspicion and worry Lya probably thought she was hiding, was going to set Cade back dramatically. It wasn't that he was trying to manipulate her, not exactly. But just that she'd learned she couldn't trust love or lovers, and he needed her to trust him.

She loved him; he was sure of it. As much as she could, anyway, and most nights, that was more than enough. He'd started out wanting her just for blood and sex, but what they had now—the connection, the companionship—was more than he'd ever dared dream of having for himself. More than he'd thought he'd be capable of as well, given how badly Morris had broken him and what had come after. And some nights, right before dawn, when he was drifting off into a sated daysleep and she was curled against his chest, a pang of fear struck him that what they had wasn't enough for her to want to stay with him forever. Or as much of forever as she'd have without him trying to turn her.

The risk that he might once more end up broken scared the bloody daylights out of him, even as he craved more of anything Lya would give him.

He wouldn't stop her from leaving if she wanted. But these last few months had shifted something in him. Where once he'd sought power and safety in solitude, what he wanted now was as much of forever as he could get with her, not just for her blood but for her company. That was a him problem, not one he'd ever force on her.

But he also wouldn't deny what he wanted in his own damn head and heart...and loins, of course. Not to mention his stomach.

Sighing, he fought off the pull to go back to sleep. This far south, the sun made him grouchier than it had farther north, but if he didn't say something now, Lya would likely spend the next few hours puttering around, doing odd chores and coming up with her own explanations. She might even take off, as she had a few times, rather than hashing something out with him directly. Her natural suspicion and reticence kept her alive as a bounty hunter, but also kept him on his toes.

"Ly," he said.

She glanced up from where she'd folded herself in the old armchair, her dark eyes wary.

He gave himself a moment just to enjoy looking at her. Her tight, dark curls were frizzed with sleep and humidity, but he loved them. Her brown skin had darkened with the Florida sun, taking on a reddish undertone that wasn't sunburn, and her lean form was accentuated by just enough curve to fill his hands. When he drank from her, sometimes he thought she tasted like sunlight used to feel.

He couldn't lose her. Not over Alejandro.

Her arched eyebrow reminded him to finish explaining. "It's not that I was trying to hide this from you."

"I know." The lopsided smile she mustered had a little pain in it. "You don't owe me explanations, Cade. I know you're over there trying to figure out how not to make me run. I won't. I just…I don't know. He was kind of a lot."

"Okay. If you want to know, you can ask."

Lya made herself smaller. "It's more that I suspect this is what Callista's job is. It's all too coincidental."

"Mmm." That had occurred to him as well, and if Alejandro was crawling out of his hole, odds were good he wasn't the only one. There were items in this particular treasure hoard that would be dangerous in the wrong hands. Hands like Alejandro's, given the witch used blood magic and would happily dabble in the soul magic forbidden by the Détente. Not all blood magic was bad. But soul magic? There was a reason it was banned under the rules governing Otherside.

Cade loved Lya deeply, but she had turned on him once—and once was enough to remind him of the lesson he'd learned under Morris's cruel hands. She'd made it up to him or they wouldn't be here, but it'd been her debt to Callista that'd tipped the scales against him before. He needed to play this one cautiously, as much to keep her from running as to stay ahead of Callista and her damn debts.

"If it comes to it, can we trust him?" Lya asked.

"No." Cade wasn't going to mince words. "Alejandro is…complicated. He was a witch, once. Much quieter about it than he is now, given the Inquisition then. But he was also a Conquistador, and the fuckery of that time gave him space to do some evil shit by the standards of both now and then, shit he could get away with when the Spanish colonized this side of the world. From what I've gathered, the witches tried and failed to Sever him when he left the Way and started misusing blood magic. He has his own twisted sense of honor, but he serves himself first and foremost now."

"A Conquistador?" Lya frowned, eyes skyward. "But that was—"

"Roughly during my original time period, yes." He shifted, trying to get comfortable, because he was crashing fast as the sun rose higher, despite taking her blood last night. "If he could have found a djinni willing to help back then, I don't doubt he would have become a lich. But he didn't have the patience to keep looking. Stolen shapeshifting and blood magic fueled by torture and murder were enough for what he wanted while extending his life and catering to his particular tastes."

She pulled a face, looking disgusted and sick. "Oh."

"If it comes down to it, we'll work with him purely because it's better than having him at our backs. But Ly? Don't ever, ever let him get you alone."

Her wide eyes told him that for once, she understood and appreciated the magnitude of the danger. As sleep pulled him back under, she moved from the chair to the bed with stealthy movements. When she was close, he caught her in a last burst of energy and pulled her tight against him with a small growl of pleasure.

"Love you," he said.

"Love you too."

The sad note in her voice worried him, but the sun weighed heavier. Right as he lost himself to it, her phone chirped, and she stiffened against him.

Callista's tone.

He let her go, wrestling to stay awake. It was entirely possible, but the strength of the sun here made him groggy and slow unless he exerted a significant force of will or drank far more blood than a town this size could reasonably sustain without notice. How the Miami coterie functioned, he couldn't imagine.

"Shit," Lya said.

Cade forced his eyes back open, already dreading the long day this was about to become.

"She wants me back in the Triangle. By tomorrow night." She winced. "And she's pissed I didn't acknowledge her last text."

"What's the job?"

"Still hasn't said. But let's assume it's the treasure. Changing the terms of my exile had to have cost her something, and with us killing Morris, she never got the payoff she was expecting. So now it's going to come out of my skin, one way or another."

He grimaced. "That doesn't give me a lot of time to arrange renewed guest rights with Torsten's coterie."

"Even if you could, Callista's banished you. This doesn't say anything about you coming back. Just me."

That did present a problem. In most other territories, the reigning Master of the City or their second would be the one who had a say in whether Cade, a declared vagabond, could travel freely in their territory and drink from their herd. But the Triangle was an outlier, governed by a triumvirate consisting of not only Torsten as Master of the City of Raleigh but also of the elven Conclave of Queens in Chapel Hill and the joined leopard and jaguar wereclans of Durham. Above them all sat the factionless hag Cade had disliked ever since he first visited North Carolina with Morris, before it was North Carolina: Callista.

It grated on him that Lya was indebted to her. More than grated. Infuriated him. But a debt was a debt. They'd wiggled out of the first one by colluding. This time would be harder.

He'd find a way. She was his. He was keeping her. That was that. And maybe, just maybe, there was a way to salvage this situation.

She read it in some shift of his expression. "Cade…" Some of her earlier reticence melted as she returned to him yet again, pushing him to his back and straddling him. "You won't always be able to save me."

"I'm not trying to save you. As I recall, you're the one who saved *me*." He forced a grin and put a finger over her lips to forestall the coming protest that she'd attacked him first. He'd forgiven her for that. Mostly. "I'm trying to make sure we can continue our beach getaway as quickly as possible. You smell too good when you've been out in the sun and the waves."

Shifting his hand to the back of her head, he pulled her down for a kiss.

Lya relaxed against him, and Cade flipped her, lavishing her body with kisses until she giggled and momentarily forgot Callista, North Carolina, and the debts waiting for her there.

And all the while, he worked on a plan to join her. Because he didn't trust for a second that Callista or Lya's cousins in House Monteague were going to make this job easy for her, and he couldn't allow certain items, or Lya herself, to fall into the wrong hands. Nor would he trust anyone with the secret of what was in the treasure. If Lya knew, she might be forced to tell Callista, and that simply wouldn't do. Lya would be pissed if she found out he'd been hiding more shit from her, but she was his to protect and he'd be damned if he sat back and did nothing.

***

She left before dawn. Cade held his tongue as she packed her weapons and a suitcase into her vehicle, the same Ford Escape they'd fled North Carolina in three months ago. This was her obligation, and however much he hated it, he admired her for facing it head on, despite the low tang of fear he could smell on her.

"Travel safely," he murmured after kissing her deeply. More sternly, he added, "And don't let the fucking Monteagues goad you into anything. I'll be too far away to be pulling bullets out of you."

She winced but didn't deny they'd try. "I'll let you know when I'm in Durham."

"Be sure you do, love."

After another kiss and a lingering hug that felt like she was trying to meld her body into his, she fled, sniffling and swiping quickly at her face.

Shit. She'd never cried that he'd seen, not even when she'd been shot. She was the toughest little thing he'd ever encountered, but this was upsetting her that much. He could flatter himself to think it was about being separated from him, but he could still scent her as she hurried away and into the car. It was frustration. Rage. If he knew her at all, it was all tied up in the circumstances of her exile to this land.

Damn Callista and damn the Lyon Conclave of Queens— even if their exiling her was what had sent her into his path and made her his.

Lya flashed him an artificially bright smile and a wave as she got in the car. Then it was just him in the predawn light, watching the taillights recede as she pulled through the gate and onto the road.

She'll be fine. She can handle herself. And I'll be the backup plan.

There was no way in hell Cade was going to wait here in Florida while Callista tried to make a tool or a corpse out of Lya five hundred miles away.

He had a restless slumber and was up again just as the sun was setting. He wanted to hunt today in case he wouldn't be able to later, but first he needed to talk to Alejandro about his backup plan. Having faith in Lya's ability to handle herself didn't mean that he couldn't lay a parallel plan in motion just to be safe.

The turnskin slunk out of the brush in coyote form this time, a shape borrowed from one of the many bones clacking around the beast's neck. He must have changed inside the fence line at the back. It was unlikely a coyote ranging through town would go unremarked in St. Augustine, unless he had another spell that made them overlook him as a stray dog.

"She's not here for you to impress, Alejandro," Cade said softly.

With a disappointed huff, the coyote trotted to the porch steps and shifted to become a naked and completely unabashed man. "Shame. I liked her."

That put Cade on alert, although he suppressed his natural defensive inclination to bare fangs. "Mind you don't like her too much. I'd hate for us to have to have a rematch."

Alejandro smirked as he climbed the steps, let himself into the lanai, and dropped into one of the chairs. "So. What say you on my plan?"

Cade leaned back in his chair, steepling his fingers and settling into vampiric stillness. Alejandro stiffened by degrees as Cade thought through what he was about to propose for the tenth time since it'd occurred to him. "I'll bite." He smiled, intentionally showing fangs this time in an unsubtle threat. "For now. I have reason to believe there are additional parties in search of that treasure."

"Oh? Why's that?"

"Because if my guess is correct, they just hired my lady to get it for them."

A crafty leer twisted Alejandro's lips. "I'm surprised at you, Cade. You'd undercut your own woman?"

"A means to an end." Cade let the half-truth sink in. It certainly was a means to an end, just not the one Alejandro would assume. The man always thought the worst of others because of the things he himself had done and would do again without qualm. "I have terms."

"Let's hear them then."

"My lady, the one you met here yesterday, is untouched. I don't care what she does—you don't lay a body part, a spell, a tool, a weapon, or a single round of ammunition on her. You take neither blood nor bone, hide nor hair, aura nor soul. Not the smallest or most ephemeral piece of her. You don't claim or twist or do magic upon her person, name, birthdate or time, or birthplace." He'd learned to be very specific and was rewarded by Alejandro's mood souring.

Liked her, indeed. Liked the prospect of harvesting parts from one of the elf-blooded, more like—especially one like Lya. The half-human were fair game as far as most predatory Othersiders were concerned, Cade included.

His stomach turned at making a deal with this asshole, but he hadn't been able to find another way around the situation. Not with him being banished.

After letting that settle, Cade continued. "You provide transport and funding."

"Now wait a minute—"

"Shut up. If there was anyone else who knew where Morris hid his shit, you'd have gone to them rather than lucking out on my coming back to town after fifty years and staying long enough for you to hear about it. No?"

Alejandro glared.

"I thought so. Do we have a deal?"

"My cut is fifty percent."

"Your cut is thirty percent, or you can fuck right off into the sea."

Another long glare. "Fine. What's going to stop you from telling her where the treasure is?"

"Oh, I fully intend on telling her. Eventually." When he'd removed the more dangerous items to hide again, he'd hand the rest of it over to Lya himself, even if she'd be pissed about all of this.

Fury twisted Alejandro's features. "Then what—"

"Nobody can open the chest containing the treasure without me. It's spelled. With Morris dead, I'm the only one who knows how." He watched the turnskin work through that.

It was clear Alejandro had thought of a way to circumvent Cade when he smiled obligingly and extended a hand. "Very well. Thirty percent. No harm to your woman. I provide transport and funds. You provide location and equal share of protection."

"Done."

They shook on it.

"We leave in two hours." Alejandro rose and slipped out of the lanai. "Meet me at the fort."

Cade gave him an annoyed look through the screen.

He chuckled. "What? You might have had a shitty time there, but it's convenient."

"Fine. The fort in two hours."

With a nod and a cat-like grin, Alejandro clutched the talon hanging from one of the leather thongs around his neck, murmured a few words, and shifted into a hawk that spread his wings and took off, easily clearing the thick foliage.

Cade just scrubbed his hands over his face and tried to figure out how the hell he was going to square this with Lya. Good intentions only went so far. But her cousins were rumored to have a way to read memories Aetherically and Callista had that torture chamber in the bar's basement, so Cade was left playing both ends against the middle and praying she'd forgive him when the bodies hit the floor.

Because with him, Lya, Callista, Alejandro, and who the hell knew who else involved, they certainly would.

Chapter 4: Lya

North Carolina wasn't exactly home, but it was the closest I had to it on this side of the ocean just for pure familiarity. It felt good to be back in the Triangle, even if my stomach was knotted with dread at seeing Callista again and my lunch wanted to come back up. I had time before sundown, but there was no way I was fucking around with Callista's timeline by sorting out a hotel. Besides, I was hoping she'd do the decent thing and spring for lodgings, since she'd summoned me back up here on such short notice. Odds were good she wouldn't, but without knowing what the job was, there was no point anyway.

I parked in the gravel-and-dirt lot in front of the bar, slumping against the driver's seat to give myself a minute after the long drive. I'd call Cade later, when I'd had the damn meeting and was lodged somewhere safe. No need to give him false hope if Callista was just going to kill me on entering the bar. I missed him already, but I needed to focus on the job. Besides, I hadn't quite managed to sort out what he might be hiding from me. Yeah, he'd explained Alejandro. Partially. But what had he been doing in company with a blood witch of that reputation? How much more was he hiding?

With a deep breath, I set it aside, got my mind in order, and reminded myself that running wouldn't fix this. Callista might not have Watchers everywhere, but she had connections. And even if I wasn't entirely sure what game Cade was playing, I refused to let my debts hurt him.

The bar was the same godsforsaken space it always had been, deceptively warm with wood paneling and low lighting. The framed Tarot cards on the wall gave it away though—whatever mission of vengeance Callista was on.

Another woman was already at the bar, getting the sharp side of Callista's tongue from the look of it. I didn't recognize her from my last visit here. Newcomer, maybe. She was a little darker than my tawny brown skin tone with tighter curls bouncing in abundance to her shoulders and some kind of bird-and-wind tattoo showing through the tank top straps on her back. She almost looked like one of my cousins from back home, enough that I barely stopped myself from doing a double take.

I politely ignored them both though, even though I found it strange that a magical null would be in an Otherside bar. Mundanes were supposed to be turned away by the spells in the land and building. Odd. I didn't like odd. But I couldn't place the woman's faction, and if Callista was in her business, I didn't want it to be any of mine.

Callista flicked a glance at me before turning back to her other guest. "Get out. Don't disappoint me." Without waiting for a response, she turned to me. "At least someone in this backwater understands their obligations." She looked behind me at the door. "And is clever enough not to bring troublesome partners with her."

I flushed, missing Cade all over again. "Just me. As ordered."

"Good. Very good. My office."

I followed her through the door to the back then into her office. This time, I took the seat she offered, preferring to be obliging if it'd keep her more agreeable with me than she'd been with the null.

She stared at me for long enough that I wondered if I'd made a mistake. Then she said, "Your stunt with Morris cost me a great deal."

That wasn't a question, so I kept my mouth shut.

"Fortunately for you, it also opened an opportunity. As does your little dalliance with Cade."

Again, not a question, although I couldn't quite suppress a grimace. Of course she knew. She'd had three months to put together whispers of secrets and truths. With an effort, I pushed away a spike of fear. Just because Henri had abandoned me when our secret had gotten out didn't mean Cade would.

"I want you to fetch something for me."

I nodded. Not much else I could do. "This will clear our debt?"

"If I get what I want, yes."

I frowned. That implied that if I tried and failed, I'd still be in her debt regardless of whatever pain and effort I expended.

"I understand." I didn't agree, but I understood.

"Clever girl. Now. Morris was a pirate back when he and I were new to the colony. I want you to find his treasure and bring it to me. One thing in particular. A gem."

I feigned surprise at Morris being a pirate—easy enough with the revelation or implication that he'd been involved with Callista—and at the confirmation that I was indeed here to find a treasure. "A gem. Size? Color? Quality?"

"Just bring back all the gems. Preferably all of the treasure, but the gems if nothing else. I'm not stupid. I imagine you'll need to pay a few people off from the haul to get to it."

"Why's that? Ma'am." I added the last when she narrowed her eyes at me.

"Because Morris would have laid traps on it, of course, and that assumes the sirens haven't gotten their claws on it."

I went cold, and not just for the stray thought whispering that Cade had to have known some of this and said nothing. "Sirens. This far north."

The water here got a little too chilly to support sirens, or so I would have thought. They were deadly dangerous and capricious as hell. This would complicate the job immensely.

She nodded, green eyes glittering as though daring me to object.

I didn't. "Got it. Traps. Sirens, which means it's at the coast." That squared with what Cade had said about the Outer Banks, at least. "Any other Otherside factions?"

"A few witches. The odd sea fae from time to time. Nothing organized—or at least, there had better not be."

Chewing my lower lip, I thought it over. If not for the sirens, I'd say the job sounded too easy to be worth clearing my debt. But sirens were trouble, and cursed treasure was trouble. And so was this hint that there might be someone out at the coast organizing sea fae within Callista's territory without her blessing. If the curse or spell was on the container, I could simply bring it back and let Callista deal with it. But if the spell was embedded in the container's resting place or the treasure itself, that was another matter.

Then it occurred to me that she might know where it was and how to reverse any spells if she and Morris had history, but Cade would as well, sending that little seed of doubt into sprouting.

When she saw I'd figured that out, she said, "I don't want Cade back in the state. If you can get information from him, fine. But if I find out he's returned, I'll tell Torsten that he killed his own master, and you can see how that works out for you. If you can convince Cade to stay away, I'll throw in a ten percent cut of whatever you bring back, on top of clearing your debt." She smiled knowingly. "I'm sure it'd be enough that you don't have to rely on him."

I hesitated. It wasn't that I *minded* living in Cade's house and eating food he bought and paying for things with his cash. I was fine with it.

Or I would be if I wasn't currently so dependent on him, having had to leave behind everything that wouldn't fit in my car when we'd fled the Triangle back in June, after already having done the same thing just eight months prior. I kept losing, except for Cade. He'd chosen me, and I'd chosen him.

And of the two of us, I was the one who'd lost more, even if I'd gained someone who loved me. It seemed silly and petty to compare but still. I liked my independence. I wanted at least the illusion that I could make it on my own if I had to, and right now, I didn't have that because there were so few Othersiders in the Jacksonville-St. Augustine area that bounty work had been sparse. I needed *something* for myself.

Callista read the conflict on my face. "I thought so." She slid a folded paper across the desk. "Go here. I'll provide more information tomorrow."

"You want me to leave now?" I spluttered before I could stop myself. "I just drove seven and a half hours to get here."

Again, the narrow-eyed glare. I didn't back down. I was tapped out after my new moon activities with Cade and a long, stressful drive.

"Your travel arrangements are not my problem. Time is of the essence. You'll go tonight, or you'll be in breach of our agreement." She rose, signaling the end of this meeting. "I don't have time to waste, girl."

I slumped, already bone-tired but not seeing a way out of this. And she hadn't said anything about lodgings at the coast, although maybe that was on the piece of paper I hadn't looked at yet. Gritting my teeth, I reminded myself where I was and, more importantly, who I was here.

That was, exactly nobody. A solo, exiled nobody, at that.

Durham was part were territory and part neutral ground. Callista was nasty enough that, if I pushed, she'd probably put me up in a hotel on the RTP side of town, where my elven cousins would be free to take a crack at me. Of course, she'd call it getting me closer to getting on the road, but we both knew.

She smiled sharply when I nodded. "Excellent. Welcome back, my dear. For now. If you need anything before your departure, find one of the witches or weres. Contact information for Janae and Terrence are on that paper."

I took it and rose slowly, tucking it into my pocket as I inclined my head, speaking the formal words that would bind us both. "I honor my debts. So one is called, so it shall be paid."

"Good girl. Off you go."

It irked me that she hadn't offered the ritual part *she* was supposed to say, but Callista always did things her own way and I didn't have the power to insist. I made my way back outside choking on resentment and drove over to the burger and brewery place on Parrish in the city center. I had no idea how much farther I'd be driving tonight. The coast was anywhere from two to five hours away and, assuming it was the Outer Banks, it'd be on the long end of that. She'd only said leave today, not how late.

The weather had cooled down since I was here last, some of the humidity giving way to the slightly drier climes of early autumn. It'd be nice to sit outside and enjoy it while I uncramped my legs. Pretend that life was normal for a minute, before throwing myself into a cursed treasure hunt.

Cade wouldn't be up yet, so I sent a quick text that I'd arrived in Durham and would call later then sorted myself out with a pimento burger, sweet potato fries, and a lemonade and enjoyed the sun. Distant music spoke of a street performer somewhere, and at the next table, a group of youths argued about the increasing cost of living in the city as it gentrified.

Yeah. Good to be back. Even under the circumstances.

When I'd finished my burger, I opened the paper Callista had given me, blowing out a sigh of relief when I spotted the address of a hotel. It'd been booked starting tonight—presumptuous of her, but she had all the power. Relief turned into a groan at the location: Hatteras Island, one of the more distant in the string of barrier islands off the main coast of the state to the east. Another six hours driving. I was definitely going to need some witch magic to make it.

Beyond annoyed, I dialed the number for Janae. After a quick introduction and an explanation of what I needed, she told me to stay put. Another witch would bring what I'd asked for.

I ordered another lemonade while I waited and picked at my fries, debating whether I wanted to get a second burger for the road and planning my route. That took all of five minutes though, which left me plenty of time to think about Cade. How much I missed him. How much he frustrated me just now. Wondering if that meant I really was a glorified pet and not a girlfriend. Still, more than anything, I missed his quiet presence and outrageous stories.

Another twenty minutes passed before a middle-aged woman with a cloud of curly hair and light brown skin approached. "Room for a friend from the other side of town?"

I looked up and smiled, as though we were indeed old friends. She'd slipped "other side"—Otherside—into her question, which meant this was my witch contact. "Hey! Good to see you. Always space for a friend."

She settled onto the bench next to me and leaned in like we were gossiping girlfriends. "I'm Hope. I've got a shop around the corner. Momma called and said you needed a pick-me-up," she murmured when she was seated. She studied me. "We don't get many of you in this part of the Triangle."

"For good reason. My cousins and the Arbiter are both inclined to give me trouble."

"Understood. How much of a boost do you need?"

I sighed. "I spent the day driving up here from Florida, and now she's sending me to the Outer Banks. Tonight. I need to be able to handle trouble on the other end."

Hope winced. "Tall order but okay. Your hand?"

I gave it to her, and with a quick glance around, she took it and murmured a few words, half prayer to the Goddess and half invocation. My eyes widened as some of the potted plants wilted and my earlier exhaustion fled, leaving me feeling like I'd had a full night of good sleep.

Frowning, the witch released my hand. "It's not just the drive. You're dehydrated, and your blood volume is lower than I'd expect."

"I, ah—my boyfriend is…"

"Got it." She fished in the big boho-style crossbody bag she'd set on the bench next to her, filling a small paper packet with what looked like homemade herbal pastilles from a larger packet. "Take one each of the round and oblong ones when you get where you're going. Take this now."

She dropped a round one in my palm.

I took it with lemonade and then accepted the packet, slipping it into my own purse. "Thank you. This helps a lot. How much do I owe you?"

"Don't worry about it. Callista will cover it."

"Thanks twice then. Can I get you a drink at least?"

The witch started to shake her head then shrugged. "You know what? Sure. The beer's good here."

We made small talk while waiting for that then a little more as we left. When she turned off to return to her shop, she said, "Be careful, Lydia. The Arbiter's been extra prickly lately. I don't know if this has to do with it, but you strike me as someone who likes to play with fire. Don't. Not this time."

"Got it. Thanks again."

Hope waved and made her way down the small side street, her long cotton skirt flapping and sandals slapping with the speed of her pace. I headed back to my car, mentally steeling myself for another long drive and the challenges waiting on the other end of it.

That, and what I was going to tell Cade.

Chapter 5: Lya

Night caught me still on the road, so it was well past Cade's waking hour by the time I'd arrived in the Outer Banks, found my hotel on Hatteras Island, secured the room to my satisfaction, and collapsed on the bed. I wanted to go to sleep, but I pulled out my phone and called Cade. It rang longer than I would have expected, knowing he would have been worried. Was he mad at me for insisting he stay behind? That didn't seem like him. Had that Alejandro come back? Was he in danger?

He finally picked up. "Hey, there you are. You're okay?"

"I'm fine," I said. "Callista sent me on another drive as soon as I got here. Outer Banks. I've only just arrived. Are you okay?"

"Hekate be praised," he said. "I'm fine. Busy but fine."

"Do you have a minute now?"

"For you? Always."

I smiled. Then it faded as Callista's demand came to mind. I wrestled with how much to tell him then settled on all of it. I couldn't go on keeping things from him when I wanted him to be open with me. "Cade…we were right. She wants me to find Morris's treasure. But there was a stipulation to the job. A catch, I guess."

"What's that?" The protective growl in his voice almost made me smile again.

"She explicitly stated she wants you to stay out of the territory. The whole state."

"Does she now?" The growl dipped an octave, becoming dangerous. "Why is that?"

"I don't know. But she threatened to tell Torsten that you killed Morris if she finds out you're here."

He let that stew. "She also knows I know where the treasure is and how to recover it."

"Yep."

"So, she must be assuming I have a motivation to keep it for myself, rather than turn it in to buy out your debt. Which would be easiest for everyone involved." He paused, and when I didn't disagree, he added, "What else does she want?"

I grimaced. It really could be that easy, but the debt was mine and Callista didn't want it to be that easy. Just like with the elves, I had to be seen to be working it off. Still, something about that seemed off. Callista valued efficiency. As long as she got what she wanted, what the hell did it matter if Cade helped?

"She wants a gem," I said slowly, still thinking. "She didn't say anything about it. I'm just to bring everything back. But I'm really wondering if there's another layer to this. Like maybe..."

"What?"

"Like maybe I'm not really supposed to come back from this job," I whispered. "She said there were sirens. She threatened you. And we both know she'd have no problem playing multiple sides and, say, turning me over to the Monteagues if they're still complaining about me disrespecting Farand."

My former boss was a bigoted asshole who'd pushed me into mouthing off, which had given him the excuse he'd needed to send thugs from House Monteague to shoot me as a reminder of my place in the local Otherside community.

I shuddered at the memory. I was fine alone. I really was. Mostly. For one of the elf-blooded, anyway; we thrived in company with others and suffered without it. I'd hunted alone for a decade, but all of a sudden I wished Cade could be here.

Whatever was going on with us, being with him would be better than dealing with this sudden feeling of being set up for another fall alone.

I dragged my knackered brain back on target and thought fast, trying to put the pieces together. There had to be a reason why this was being made unnecessarily difficult. "Callista knows we're together. She knows I'm good on my own, but with a five-hundred-year-old vamp at my back? That gives me decent odds against most of Otherside unless they come in numbers. Numbers she won't have in the Outer Banks or who won't be as loyal to her as those directly under her thumb in the Triangle."

Cade sighed. "I don't like this. I really, really don't like this."

"I know. Me neither. But let's play along for now, okay? I can't afford to be on her bad side again."

"We'll both do what we must."

I frowned and tried not to be suspicious about that phrasing. "Good. Did Alejandro come back?"

"Yes, in fact. We're out together now, hashing a few things out."

"Oh. Shit. Sorry, if I'd known you were busy with him I'd have—"

"Don't worry. I should get back to him though, before he does something foolish. Stay safe, okay?"

"You too. Love you."

"And I you."

I hung up, stomach churning. Something about that conversation didn't sit right with me. Maybe it was just the idea of Cade "hashing things out" with the turnskin he'd already said he didn't trust. Might have been my new suspicion that Callista had more than one game afoot now. Whatever it was, I had to give him the benefit of the doubt. The oddness might just be that he'd been with Alejandro and couldn't speak freely.

The boost Hope had given me earlier was wearing off. I downed the little tablets she'd given me, took a quick shower, and went to bed, still wondering what the catch was in all this. The crash of waves reminded me of home with Cade in Florida, and I finally fell asleep.

Tired as I'd been, I was still up at dawn—both because of my nature and because I didn't want to miss an instruction from Callista. The hotel stay was on her tab, so I got the breakfast buffet and loaded up with sausage, bacon, eggs, and a small bowl of fruit for good measure. A cup of black coffee with sugar and a glass of orange juice rounded me out. I sat on the deck and watched the sun rise over the ocean, lulled by the rhythmic motion of the water. We had the Rhône and Saône rivers in Lyon, placid and channeled by the city on their banks, and the Thames in London. Nothing like this. I'd seen the ocean once before moving in with Cade, and I could see why he'd turned pirate to stay with it.

The meal went a long way toward rejuvenating me, but it sat poorly in my stomach when my phone announced a text from Callista.

Get to Ocracoke. Springer's Point. Send me a picture when you're there.

I sighed, rolling my eyes as I pushed the remains of my breakfast away. Why had she booked me a room on Hatteras if I needed to be on Ocracoke? Did she not really know where the treasure was? Or was this to do with more Othersiders?

Another text came through. *Today, Desmarais.*

"Bloody hell, as though I want to be here any longer than I have to be," I muttered. I stalked back to my room to find my laptop and make my plan. My earlier pleasure at the sunrise fled as though it'd washed out with the tide.

First job was to figure out how the hell to get to Ocracoke. Ferry, apparently, and I frowned at the map showing the circuitous route it took through sandbars and around a crab spawning sanctuary. This whole area was prime siren territory—shoals, the sound between the barrier islands and the mainland, plenty of bays and estuaries. They liked dangerous or changeable waters with a small human population to toy with, and I had a feeling this area rearranged itself after every hurricane. I still thought it was too cold for them to want to stay year-round, but maybe they were migratory or had simply adapted.

In any case, once on Ocracoke, I'd need to find somewhere to park for the day. I could simply take the passenger ferry rather than inconvenience myself with my car, but I didn't fancy being reliant on alternative transportation. Springer's Point was a nature preserve on the opposite end of Ocracoke from the ferry, accessible by foot traffic only, which would be a pain in the ass for carrying treasure out. I had no idea how much there was or how much of it was gems or how heavy it'd be. That assumed it was even in the same place Callista thought it was. With all the hurricanes that must have hit the coast between whatever century Morris had hidden it and now, it could well have shifted—and that was if Morris hadn't simply moved it himself.

From there, I had no idea. I'd take a rucksack with me, but today was just going to be a recon day. I couldn't be expected to do everything all in one day when I hadn't even been given full instructions about what I was supposed to be finding, where, or how.

I leaned back in my chair, trying to think it through. Cade had said Morris had killed his other fledglings, so whatever it was should be manageable by no more than two people. Then again, those two people had been vampires—stronger than human and stronger than me as well, and that's assuming glamoured humans hadn't been used as pack mules. But they'd likely have been traveling at night, over rough terrain. Vampires could see well in the dark even by starlight and were more agile, but they were still limited by shit like gravity and tripping over unseen rocks and roots. So maybe it wouldn't be that big.

Of course, I could always just ask Cade.

I picked up my phone, bouncing it in my hand. Something about our call last night had rubbed me wrong. I couldn't put my finger on it, but he'd sounded cagey in a way he hadn't since we'd left the Triangle. It might simply have been having to deal with Alejandro. It was clear there was bad blood there, and Cade wouldn't have liked the other man's interest in me. But my instincts said it was something else.

He wouldn't come up here, would he? Not after I'd explained what was going on, told him Callista's threat, and explicitly asked him not to?

I sighed.

He might. He really just might, driven by a vampiric possessiveness and a protective streak I loved but would cause us problems if he followed it now. I swiped a text message out: *Please tell me you're not planning to come up. And if there's something I need to know about the treasure—*

No. I erased all of it.

He was coming up, or he wasn't. If he wasn't, I didn't need to look mistrustful. If he was, I'd deal with him when he got here. Instead, I took a sexy selfie when I changed into my bikini to look more like a tourist and sent it with a short voice message: "Stay out of trouble. I love you."

That done, I dressed in green camo shorts and a grey T-shirt, tucked my curls under a darker grey cap, and put on some sneakers for all the walking the day was going to require. I still had a concealed carry permit for North Carolina, so I threw my Walther PPK in my purse alongside a steel bottle of water, a packet of jerky, and my Leatherman multi-tool. The gun was the smallest one I owned and only had seven shots, but if I had to use it rather than bluffing my way out or using Aether to mindmaze someone, I had much bigger issues. I tucked the purse itself inside the rucksack, wanting my hands free. A pair of aviator sunglasses and I was good to go.

The hour-long ferry ride gave me time to brush up on siren lore. I'd never had to hunt one, and I prayed this wouldn't be the day I started. Human stories on the internet overlapped with Otherside knowledge in a few key areas, namely the singing. I made a mental note to stop by a pharmacy or something and get some earplugs before going out to the water. Or to the water alone, anyway, given that I was already on the ferry. This trip was the first I'd heard of sirens on this coast, which meant there were probably few enough they wouldn't bother with a boat this size.

I just hoped I wouldn't have to go anywhere in a motorboat.

Once we docked, I made my way into town. Found a place to park and then a small shop that had the earplugs I wanted. It was late morning by the time I got to where I was supposed to be and sent Callista a picture of the trail head. Her response came back immediately.

Find the old cistern.

Annoyed, I did as she said. It wasn't far, an easy walk, but unfortunately, there were other tourists. I joined them, taking a photo both to blend in and to prove to Callista I was following her asinine instructions.

Twenty paces south.

I waited until the family had moved on then did as she said, remembering Morris's height being close to Cade's and lengthening my paces accordingly. Then backed up and did it again, considering how short Callista was. Fuck it. At this point, it was all ridiculous. I took a picture of the spot, wondering how the fuck Callista would recognize anything, but she just kept sending instructions until I was standing in front of a broken tree with "MORRIS" carved high up into it in letters that were so weathered they were nearly gone.

"Well I'll be damned," I muttered.

My phone buzzed. *Dig.*

I frowned, not having brought anything to dig with but not daring to tell Callista that. For lack of any better options, I grabbed a broken tree branch and picked it through the sandy soil, growing hotter and more annoyed by the minute. Had Cade been out here like this? The heat shifted from annoyance to something sexier when I imagined what he might have been wearing and I couldn't help a smirk despite the sweat dripping into my eyes. He'd confirmed the accuracy of the outfits I'd found on Google, and the thought of him in those billowy shirts shouldn't have been hot given how good he looked in sleek, modern, three-piece designer suits, but the man had a model's body and the gaze of an incubus. Period costume would look just as good on him as anything else, and the thought of him wielding a sword…yummy.

All my fantasizing could only distract me for so long. When I had a reasonably big hole, I sent a picture and added, *There's nothing here.*

The bitch kept me shifting here and there for another hour as I looked over my shoulder for a park ranger or another tourist who'd tell me to stop and give me an excuse to end this nonsense.

Finally, I threw down the branch and dialed, frustrated enough to dare. "It's not here."

"Then that bastard left me decoy instructions or moved it," she hissed. The connection crackled. "Go back into town. Find Mami Wata. Ask her what she knows. Tell her you're asking with my voice."

The call ended, and I glared at my phone, furious.

Who the fuck was Mami Wata? What faction and where the hell was I supposed to find her? She had to be an Othersider. But was she a witch? Or something else? Had I trespassed on territory I should have paid a forfeit to access so that Callista could get what she wanted more cheaply? Again, the whole expedition had been needlessly complicated. Why hadn't I been told about this Mami Wata to begin with? I stomped back the way I'd come, tired and sweaty but fueled by rage. The bitch was as cheap as she was corrupt.

And somehow, it broke through that Cade might have known the treasure wouldn't be here. If he had, and he'd said nothing, what did that mean for us? And what had he been hashing out with Alejandro?

My stomach twisted like I was going to hurl. Maybe I really was just a pet. I'd fooled myself before, after all.

I trusted Cade with my body and my life, but I didn't like that I was having to wonder if I could trust him with anything else.

Chapter 6: Cade

Cade leaned against the wall of his hotel room on Ocracoke, doing his best to keep his attention on staying awake in the midmorning sun and ignoring Alejandro's laughter. He was succeeding at the former, which only made him cranky, and failing mightily at the latter, which made him crankier. The fact that nothing of the island was what he remembered made him crankiest of all, and he wondered whether he'd be able to get what he'd come for quickly enough to beat Callista.

And Lya. He barely held back a wince. She'd be furious.

If she found out.

Which was why he needed Alejandro to get over himself, so they could move quickly and hopefully not need the pair of rooms they'd rented for more than one night. Cade might know better than Lya what was going on with the treasure, but that only helped them both if he could get to the damn chest and get them off this gods-forsaken island.

Alejandro caught his breath. "So, Morris moved the treasure right before you tried to kill him. You knew, and you know how to find it. And not only did you not tell your woman, you're going to take it yourself?"

Guilt spiked again, and Cade pulled his mind back from the text message she'd sent him this morning. "If she knows, she'll want to help."

Just like she had with Morris, and that had nearly ended disastrously for both of them.

He just wanted a peaceful, quiet life with her. If that meant undercutting Callista to buy her off with part of a treasure she thought she'd be getting in full, so be it. There was no reason for all of this to be so difficult, and if Lya's suspicion that she was intended to be a sacrificial pawn was correct, then he had to do whatever he could to throw off everyone involved. Beyond that, there were those damned gems. He couldn't let Callista have them. Hekate only knew what she'd use them for. Certainly nothing good.

Most importantly, Lya was his. He protected what was his, whatever the cost. He'd lost too much over the years, done too much to tarnish his soul, to let a prize like her slip through his fingers—or worse, be taken from him.

Cade spoke through gritted teeth. "If she doesn't know, then she can claim plausible deniability to Callista."

Alejandro just bent over and slapped his thigh, more cackles spilling from him as tears slid down his face and his necklaces clattered. "Oh, my friend. This is a trick beyond measure. You should have come with me to—"

"I told you, we're not talking about the past. We're not talking about anything, beyond what's strictly necessary to get this done and get the fuck out of town."

The witch calmed gradually, rubbing his face clean. "Fine. We're on Ocracoke, in this dramatically overpriced private lodging, as you demanded. Now what?"

"I go to the bank."

"The bank?"

The laughter started again, and Cade breathed deep, in through his nose and out through barely parted lips. If Alejandro had been paying attention, he'd recognize the sign of an agitated vampire and shut the hell up, but he was still on a high from whatever stimulant he'd taken to drive all night and completely lacking in restraint.

"Just the bank?" the turnskin finally said. "Why did you need me to come at all?"

With a growl, Cade whirled on him. "Because I knew if you didn't, you'd follow me anyway. I'd rather have you where I can see you."

Alejandro sobered, though his eyes still twinkled. "Cunning. Always cunning, our Cade. So. The treasure is at the bank?"

"No. But something else is. I need to get it. You need to stay here and wait for me."

"Is that so?" Narrowed eyes and lips pressed thin spoke to Alejandro's dangerous level of suspicion.

"It is. Can I trust you?"

"For now. But only because you know that, if you fuck me, I know what your bitch smells like. I know she'll be coming to this island. And I would very much enjoy—"

Rage made Cade snarl, full-fanged, as his glamour slithered free. He knew very well what Alejandro would like to do if he caught Lya alone, and some of the nasty magic he'd use toward his ends. "Don't. If you break our agreement, there will be no place you can hide from me. Morris taught me a great deal about pain. I would happily draw on those lessons to hurt you. You know who and what I used to be and how I practiced what I learned after I freed myself from him. Don't call my bluff."

"Then be back here within the hour with either the treasure or the next clue. I'm going to take a siesta." He left, slamming the door to Cade's suite behind him.

Tension wracked Cade, and he forced another breath. If anything happened to Lya...

No, nothing would happen. That was exactly why he was doing this.

Betraying her trust, a small whisper informed him.

To keep her safe from Callista and Alejandro, he argued back, before growling to himself and digging through his bags for one of the bottles of sunscreen he'd brought. When he was slathered and reeking of it, he grabbed a hat that'd shade his face and neck, put on a pair of sunglasses, and checked that he still had his wallet. Couldn't be too careful with Alejandro. Then he headed out.

He'd had a long, tiresome drive north to consider whether Morris would have moved the treasure again—or had it moved—after Cade had fled. His now-dead master might even have taken it, given he must have emptied the smaller St. Augustine cache to pay Callista whatever bribes had needed paying for him to be allowed into the territory without Torsten's knowledge. He'd settled on yes, it probably had been moved, and if anyone knew where it might be, it'd be Mami Wata.

Cade didn't know the spirit's real name or if she even had one. Only that she was loosely connected to the sirens in the area and had further links to the few local witches. Whatever she'd been when she was first blown to or dumped on these shores, she was now a sort of information broker for anything and everything the waters might share.

The stop at the bank was to get some pearls out of a safe deposit box to pay her with. He'd set it up after escaping Morris to cover just this eventuality, having liquidated just about everything from the treasures he'd recovered from Charleston and Savannah. He smiled to think of how livid Morris would have been on discovering those caches emptied to fund the financial instruments that now supported Cade's quietly wealthy lifestyle. He should have emptied all of them—Lya wouldn't be in danger now if he had—but he'd wanted something to fall back on. Just in case. The world of stocks and bonds and fiat currency was too new and ethereal for him to be fully comfortable with modern paper money or electronic wealth.

So much for that.

The bank was bigger than it had been before. A new generation of people worked in it. But they were happy enough to take him to a private room and fetch his box when he showed a few papers his lawyer had furnished. Selecting a string of flawless white pearls and a snake broach with thin chips of pearl for scales from the small fortune tucked into the box, he concluded his business and headed back to the hotel. He needed some downtime before visiting Mami Wata, and as much as it rubbed him wrong, he didn't dare test Alejandro's promise to hunt down Lya if he returned late.

Sundown pulled Cade awake with a slanting beam of light cutting through a crack in the blackout curtains. He rolled away from it and reached for Lya, frowning when he found neither her nor her scent before remembering he wasn't in St. Augustine anymore.

She'd left a voicemail though. "Hey, love. I'm still in the Outer Banks. Spent the day on Ocracoke." She heaved an irritated-sounding sigh, and Cade winced because he knew what was coming next. "The treasure is gone, or Callista's an idiot. Maybe both. Either way, she sent me to talk to someone called Mami Wata."

His guts froze.

Until she added, "The woman stonewalled me. Said something along the lines of 'death to tyrants' before chasing me off." An amused snort. "If it wasn't my ass on the line, I'd join her. Since it is, I need to figure out a workaround. Do you know of anything that might help?" The hesitation in her voice was a dagger in Cade's heart. She knew he knew something and was probably more than a little suspicious of last night's short phone call. "Only if it won't put you in a bad way though. I'm guessing you've got history in the area. Anyway, call me back when you're up. Love you, fangface."

Cade saved the message and ended the call then scrubbed his hands over his face. This was going to get very messy very quickly. Lya was a prodigious huntress. She'd find a way to get Mami Wata to talk. An internet search would give her a reasonable place to start, if she let go of her temper long enough to think it through. His plan was unraveling faster than he'd expected.

"Damn it," he muttered. He needed to call Lya back, but he needed to get ahead of her first. He could still salvage this.

Sliding out of bed, he dressed quickly, patting his pockets to make sure his gifts were still there. On his way out, he pounded on Alejandro's door.

The witch scowled at him, looking rumpled and drawn—presumably experiencing the aftereffects of whatever had kept him awake earlier.

"What?" Alejandro snapped.

"Just keeping you apprised. I got what I needed, and I'm headed out." Cade tapped his lip over a fang to indicate a hunt. "I'll be back later with info. Stay put and mind the rooms, okay?"

"Fine." The door slammed in Cade's face.

Fine. With a grin, he ducked his head and hurried out. Lya's blood still hummed in him, and he could go a little longer without a feed. But he always preferred not to push it since it was easier to keep his temper and his instincts leashed when he'd fed. Peak tourist season was nearly over, but there were still enough wide-eyed strangers and beachgoers that he should be able to manage something quick and quiet.

Mami Wata first though. If Lya had already been to see her, he was behind.

The water spirit's shop was on prime property close to Silver Lake, or it had been the last time he had been here. The little town was bigger, though many of the streets were still sandy trails branching off from the main road. Hands in his pockets, he wandered in the direction he remembered it being, slow enough to look local, even if he wanted to hurry.

He was just starting to think he'd gotten it wrong when he spotted the sign—Mami Wata's, painted in flowing script with a snake twining through the letters—in front of a small house. In spite of his worries, Cade grinned, glad to see some things never changed. He climbed the steps to the porch slowly then waited just inside the door as bells chimed.

"Be with you in a minute!" a familiar melodic voice called from the back.

"Take your time," he replied, checking for other visitors with all his senses. Nobody, although Lya's scent lingered under the frankincense and myrrh incense. The shelves and walls were filled with items ranging from gorgeously carved wood-framed mirrors and combs to handmade jewelry to figure candles and orderly packets of what Cade suspected were spell-crafting ingredients.

"It can't be." The spirit herself emerged from behind a curtain of clacking beads, looking exactly as she had two hundred years ago: skin dark and smooth as black star calla lilies, a small form as curvy as the waves in a storm, with curls even tighter than Lya's held back from her face with a flowing scarf the same turquoise of the Caribbean at noon. Ropes of pearls and shells hung from her neck, and thin gold bracelets ringed her arms. "Cade?"

"Blessings be upon you and your waters," he said softly, offering her a smile as he held up the small cotton bag he'd put his jewelry in. "I come bearing gifts."

Her eyes lit up, and her full lips widened in a smile as she shifted her head to give him a mock-scolding look. "You were always such a flatterer. Come here, child."

Cade went to her and kissed her on the cheek as her arms went around him.

"You smell like a girl who was here earlier." She leaned away, eyes narrowed. "Friend of yours?"

"Actually yes." Lya's scent in the shop had him missing her more than ever, and he pushed down a pang of loneliness even as he was pleased the water spirit could scent her on him. "But before business…" He gave her the bag with a small bow.

She took it and peered into it, making a delighted sound as she withdrew the pearls and added them to the collection already around her neck.

"What's this meant to pay for, naughty boy?" she asked as she admired the brooch.

"That friend of mine who was here earlier."

Mami Wata's head snapped up, and her eyes narrowed. "If you're working for that bitch Callista—"

"Nothing of the sort." He held up his hands placatingly. "Quite the opposite, actually. Although I would count it a favor if you forgave my friend. The half-elf. She has a temper on the best of days, and it sounds like this wasn't one of them."

Pursing her lips, the water spirit tilted her head, her eyes returning to the brooch. "For such a fine piece, I might even answer her questions."

"That, I ask you not to do. You and I both know why nobody can have that treasure. Or certain items in it."

"Agreed." Mami Wata sighed, running her thumb over the brooch before pinning it to her shirt to signal her acceptance of it. "I just wish it hadn't come up again so soon."

"It's still safe?"

"For now."

"Accessible?"

She smiled, showing teeth as sharp and curved as a python's since the magic hiding them under an illusion had no effect on the undead. "Oh no, my darling dark one. It's with my sisters, and they like the blood of those who are in between most of all.

Your friend's would be irresistible. And if the wrong people found that out, she'd be in even bigger danger than she already is, sniffing around these parts. The girl is lucky I ran her off."

If he'd had dinner before this, the blood would have fled his face. "I see."

Mami Wata could be reasoned with, charmed with respect and gifts. Sirens? They'd only accept blood and death, although he hadn't heard before that they preferred those of mixed heritage. He flashed back to Lya's suspicion that she wasn't meant to return from this trip alive and had a sudden suspicion Callista had known this fact.

And Callista wouldn't have told Lya. That meant a trap. One she'd need his help evading. He knew he'd been right to come.

Refocusing on the matter at hand, he said, "That's going to be an inconvenience."

"There's been too much development in the area. Too many human structures encroaching on the beach. Too many treasure hunters and pirate wannabes disobeying the signs warning them away from preserves." She turned away, waving for him to follow her. "Come. You look hungry. I can offer a little something for an old friend."

Somewhat relieved, Cade followed her through the bead curtain to a small kitchen. He sat at the old wooden table that dominated the room then stood right back up when she ran a knife over her wrist and held it over a goblet. "What—"

"You'll need it. My sisters won't give up this treasure so easily now that they have it, and I think you like your friend enough you won't want her blood to pay for it." Her wound closed, and she extended the cup, licking the smear from her wrist.

"I wasn't expecting something so generous. Thank you." Slowly, Cade accepted it.

He toasted her then bowed his head over the goblet to show proper reverence for her gift before drinking. It was a fraction of what he'd have taken from a human, but given the huge amount of power in her ancient blood, it'd keep him going another few days without needing another feed.

"Consider us even." She tapped the brooch. "The girl wasn't *that* annoying, and I got the sense she wasn't here of her own will." Darkness shaded Mami Wata's expression, a fury long buried that had the look of the sea in storm. "I know well what that's like."

"Your kindness is a boon and a balm for the windblown."

That brought a smile back to her face, and she pinched his cheek before settling opposite him at the table. "Now. Catch me up on your doings these last few years."

Cade did so, ensuring he wove some key information into the tale. Tourist shop aside, she made most of her living from secrets and tales—beyond that, she simply enjoyed knowing everyone's business, if in a less invasive and malicious way than Callista.

Then she described a ritual he could use to greet her sisters in a way that might win him success. It'd be dangerous, but it was better than risking Lya.

When the moon rose, he made his excuses, kissed her again on both cheeks, and headed out.

Warmth buzzed through him with the magic in the blood he'd drunk, and he smiled, feeling the sloppiness of it as he enjoyed the sea breeze as he made it back to the main strip of road cluttered with seafood restaurants and fishing supply stores.

A deadly soft demand came from just out of sight. "Let go of me."

Cade stiffened, his delight with the coastal night fleeing. He knew that voice.

Lya. She was still here on Ocracoke, someone had gone after her, and she didn't know he was just around the corner.

Chapter 7: Lya

I should have called it a day and gone back to Hatteras Island, but I was determined to get Mami Wata to talk to me. I'd found a bar and grill close enough to the water I could smell it over the mélange of fried food and beer and parked myself there for the afternoon. The last vehicle ferry back to Hatteras didn't leave until midnight, so I had plenty of time to stew and call it research.

I was still thinking about the pull of the woman's magic when full dark told me it was time to go. Most Othersiders grew more powerful at night, and if I didn't know what she was, I needed to assume she was the same. Wikipedia and Google searches had turned up a mix of information, but the only agreement was water spirit.

I had no idea what that meant and no experience with them, so I'd sleep on it. If Callista wanted obedience, she could come out and order it herself.

Still lost in thought both about what I'd read and at the tingling sensation that might be the tracking tag I'd put on Alejandro but might also be general annoyance, I took one of the smaller dirt roads back to the lot where I'd left my car this morning—then froze as the wind shifted and burnt marshmallow hit my nose instead of ocean brine.

"Stop, Desmarais," a masculine voice ordered from the shadow of some trees.

I couldn't quite make anyone out, which meant not only were they in the shadows, they were also drawing them closer to evade human eyes. Full-blood elves. The Darkwatch.

Goddess damn it.

I did as I was told and held my hands out before speaking in a voice low enough humans would miss it. "I'm here on Callista's orders."

"Oh, we know." Shadows cleared to reveal a tall, blond elf with grey eyes.

One of House Sequoyah, which meant there'd be at least two more to make a full triad with a member from each house. It also meant this was truly the Darkwatch, not rogue members of House Monteague, and if they were being this open with the magic, they'd already cleared the street and were on serious business.

Double damn.

"So what do you want?" Tension made me snappish, as did the fact that my weapons were still in the rucksack on my back. This was supposed to have been a recon day, not an ass-kicking day.

"I would assume you know."

"You know what they say about people who assume." I couldn't help myself.

His eyes narrowed at my cheekiness, and he glided closer, soundless as all full-blood elves were, until he was in my face. "Don't play games. We know about the treasure. Deliver it to us. All of it."

"Can't do that. I'm oathsworn to pay off a debt."

"You can do it. Because if you give it to us, there's no more debt. Queen Keithia will get Farand to shut up about disrespect and hire you in as a bounty hunter for House Monteague." He tilted his head, like I was being thick-headed. "You won't have to worry about Callista if the High Queen claims you."

I stared at him in utter disbelief. "That's literally not how any of this works, and we all know it."

"It's how it works when we say it is. Especially out here." In a flash, he sucker-punched me in the mouth, wrapped a hand around my throat when I reeled backward, and pushed me against one of the live oaks lining the street. "Or you can refuse and get more of this. We'll follow you, kill you when you have it in hand, and take it ourselves."

If it wasn't for the threat of Cade's vengeance, I was fairly sure their Plan B would have been Plan A. That gave me enough confidence to choke out, "Let go of me."

Sequoyah tilted his head, and his eyes narrowed dangerously as he drew his fist back again.

I swallowed and tensed to block him, having heard some of the Sequoyahs enjoyed hurting as much with their hands as with Aether that could be used to heal or kill.

"Brennan." Another male voice from another patch of shadow.

"I'll only hurt her a little," he snarled, looking far too enthusiastic at the prospect.

"We have company."

Brennan looked up and scented the night. With him distracted, I broke the grip he had on me and spun away, dropping my bag and bringing my hands up in a guard. I couldn't call for help without risking a breaking of the Détente, but I'd be damned if I didn't defend myself.

My heart stopped when Cade slid around the brush on the street corner, sticking to the cover offered by low-hanging tree limbs. Relief and consternation chased through me, but not quite surprise. I'd known something was up. Hoped I was wrong, but I kept getting proven right where my romantic choices were concerned.

"Brennan, is it?" he said when he was closer. His gaze flicked over the elf, and he took a deep inhale. "Of House Sequoyah." Another inhale. "As well as a Monteague and a Luna. A full Darkwatch triad for one half-elf? My Lya is tough, but this seems excessively unfriendly."

"You're not supposed to be here," Brennan snarled. "When we report—"

"Report what you please. It will gain you nothing. Not in time to do anything." Cade smiled to show his fangs, even as the black of his pupils filled his sclera.

I averted my gaze, keeping my focus on the Aether signatures I could sense.

This was bad, and all the more terrifying for the fact that it was happening in near-whispers.

Another sniff from Cade. "You drew blood?"

I swiped my hand under my throbbing lip, tasting metal as it came away wet. Shit. Cade was good about leaving me to handle my own affairs, but the elves had overstepped and something about him was off. Almost like he was drunk, but that didn't make any sense.

One of the shadows spoke, the same one as before. "He didn't—"

"He did," Cade said coldly, turning to me.

I knew what he wanted. It'd be a stretch, and it'd require me to publicly declare myself under his protection when A, he wasn't supposed to be here and B, I was furious with him for not telling me he was on his way. Still, he'd already claimed me, and the other two members of the triad didn't seem inclined to back off, which meant the Chapel Hill Conclave or Callista were ultimately behind this. They'd be more afraid of the queens or the Arbiter than they ever were of me. I was good, but I relied on traps and guile more than outright attack precisely because most Othersiders were stronger than me.

Cade and I could talk about it later, even if I resented feeling small just now.

"I invoke blood for blood," I said. "And allow Cade to claim it on my behalf."

When Brennan spun to me, snarling, I lashed out with a foot and caught him in the gut. No blood spilled, and it sent him stumbling back toward Cade, who caught both his hair and his gaze, then the whole damn elf as he slid under a heavy glamour.

The other two elves swore but didn't move. They knew a burgeoning omnishambles when they saw one. At their tacit acceptance, Cade grinned and sank fang, limiting himself to two quick swallows before dropping Brennan in the dirt. As the elf flopped to his side, glassy-eyed, I noted Cade hadn't bothered with his usual courtesy of healing the bite, which meant the elf would either be a week trying to hide it or stuck in his hotel room. Elves couldn't work magic on themselves, only others.

"Stay the fuck away from us both," Cade warned them. "If we're all here for the same thing, trust me when I say you'll regret pursuing it. Go home. Make your excuses. It'll go better for you than staying here, I promise you that."

Shadows fled as the pair still standing approached their decommissioned comrade and hoisted him up.

"We're not done," the one who looked like one of my Monteague cousins said.

Cade shrugged. "Fine. Your funeral. Now get."

With a last glare, the elves shambled away, supporting Brennan between them like he'd had a little too much to drink.

Which left me standing in the road scowling at Cade.

For better or worse, it was having no effect.

"Hey, love." He smiled sloppily.

I sighed and pinched the bridge of my nose. So he *was* blood drunk. It shouldn't have been the case on as little blood as he'd taken, even from a high-blood elf—or at least, I thought so.

Which meant he'd already been out hunting something else on the island. Given that there wasn't that much to hunt, human or Othersider, my bet was that he'd paid a visit to Mami Wata.

"Is she still alive?" I asked.

"Who?"

I raised my eyebrows.

"Oh. Of course. We're old friends. Had a gift exchange." Another wide, pointy smile.

"Old friends." Fury spiked twice over, first that he hadn't said something that would have been helpful to me earlier, second that he was standing in the street blood drunk enough to get sloppy with his fangs. "Put your teeth away. Now."

After a quick wince, he closed his lips.

"Where are you staying?"

He waved in a generally northeasterly direction. "Hotel on the beach."

Which was, now that I had a reason to focus on it, exactly where the tracking tag felt strongest. Sorting something out with Alejandro, indeed.

His mood grew more uncertain the longer I just stood there staring at him, torn between being grateful for the help, not thinking I'd needed it, and being upset he'd been here to offer it.

Was it logical? Nope. But that didn't matter one whit.

"Let's go," I said finally. "We need to talk."

He sighed and rubbed the back of his neck, stumbling over his own feet as he fell into step beside me then tripping over a stick so small a chihuahua could have carried it.

"Oh, for the love of the Goddess." I grabbed his arm and slung it over my shoulders to give him more support then pulled him in the direction of my car when he tried to lead me back down the road.

We didn't speak other than him muttering directions until we were at his hotel and safely locked in his room. He was a little more sober, but he still sat heavily on the bed and flopped onto his back.

I wrestled down a spike of lust and crossed my arms. "Explain."

"Can't."

"Can't or won't?"

"Ly—"

"Can't. Or won't?"

Cade heaved a sigh. "If I do, it puts you in danger. If I don't, you'll stay angry with me." He lifted his head. "What are you most angry about?"

"That you pretended like you weren't on your way up here. I know Alejandro is nearby as well. I put a tracking tag on the fucker."

As though his name was a summons, a loud knock on the door was followed by the man's voice. "Cade? Do I hear—"

I went for the door and yanked it open.

He jumped then smiled as he took in my mood, his attention lingering on my split lip. "I told him you'd find out."

"Shut up and get in here. I'm pissed with you too."

Shrugging, the turnskin passed me. Mixed musky scents followed him, as though he'd worn a few different skins recently.

When I'd shut and locked the door behind us, I stood with my back to the wall and glared at them both in equal measure. "I want an explanation. One that includes a reason why I shouldn't turn both of you over to Callista myself."

That was harsh, too harsh really. But I had to stay angry so I wouldn't be hurt Cade had trusted Alejandro more than me.

The former sat up, suddenly much more sober than he had been, and the latter winced.

Alejandro mirrored my lean against the wall nearest him, only with more of an animal's disinterested grace than my stiff anger. "Had I known that was who hired you, I might have passed on the opportunity. Might have. Some things are too good to pass up."

I turned my scowl to him even as Cade grinned smugly.

"Some things like what?" I asked.

"There's a gem—"

"Oh, for fuck's sake. Is that what the elves want as well?"

The witch perked up. "Elves? Ah." His gaze slid to Cade and twinkled as he guessed the reason for the vampire's state. "Perhaps. Maybe they're just greedy. There aren't many treasures left unclaimed, after all."

When Cade had nothing to add, I said, "So let me make sure I have this straight. Callista hires me to find a treasure. Cade knows not only what it is but also where and has contacts in the area, which is presumably why she didn't want him here, even if it would have made my life easier for everyone to tell me what the hell was going on." I paused to glare at him again before continuing. "You, Alejandro, know enough about the treasure to know what's in it but not where it is. I'm assuming you're here because you can't be trusted."

Unbothered, he shrugged. "A fair assessment."

"The elves have caught wind of all this somehow and want a cut. They also wouldn't mind giving me another kick while I'm down, so bonus deal for them. Which leaves me with one question, Cade. Why not just tell me what's going on?"

"Because then you'd be even more of a target for Callista," he said heavily. "Believe me when I say you don't want to be in her dungeon." His face was a little too blank, and I realized he was trying to keep Alejandro from seeing how much he cared about me. Words spoken on the phone could just be words— lies, even—but if it looked like more than that, I was leverage.

Goddess damn them both for making me play along.

Suddenly, I was too tired for this and didn't want to deal with it anymore.

"Fine. I'm calling it a night." I turned to go then raised my fist defensively when a tight grip closed around the other wrist.

Cade let me go but just looked at me.

"Don't even think of asking me to leave before updating me on your dealings today," Alejandro said, straightening.

Annoyance flickered across Cade's face, lips pressed to a thin line and brow pinched before he smoothed it. "The treasure isn't where it's supposed to be. The sirens have it."

For the first time I'd seen, Alejandro lost his swagger, shifting to thoughtfulness then avarice then a blank stillness that frightened me. "I see."

The drop in my stomach at the idea that he might be plotting something involving sirens made me sick. It was one thing for the sea fae to be in the area. It was another entirely for them to be in possession of the treasure, and yet another thing to have a blood witch Alejandro's age pretending to be disinterested in their existence.

I hated this. All of it.

Cade sighed. "I propose we all sleep on it and reconvene with ideas next sundown."

"Until sundown then." Alejandro's agreement came a little too easily, but neither Cade nor I said anything as he inclined his head and headed for the door. "Don't do anything without me." He turned and ran his gaze down my body then back up in a way that made me shudder with revulsion and want to vomit. "Or our little deal is null and void, Cade."

"Good night, Alejandro," he said coldly.

With a last smirk, the witch let himself out.

I started to follow him.

"Lya, don't run."

The desperation in his voice stopped me, but I stayed where I was, arms crossed and head down. Henri, my ex, had said those words to me once. I'd heard a rumor that someone knew about us and told him we should break it off. He'd said not to run. That I could trust him. That he loved me and he'd stand by me no matter what the queens said.

Now Cade was saying it.

If my love life went sideways again, I had nowhere else to go, and I was trapped on this godsforsaken island, smothered by my debts, and cornered by the Darkwatch. I'd be worse off than I was the first time. My heart pounded, and I squeezed my eyes shut, fighting back the urge to just go. If I left now, I might be able to get to the mainland and flee Callista's territory before she could send bounty hunters after me.

And then what? Be in exile alone again? Elves, even the half-human, were intensely social. I needed *someone*, or I'd go mad. Literally mad—the hormone imbalance would wreck me if it went on for too long, which made me wonder if Callista separating Cade and me had been part of the punishment for fleeing with him.

Elves needed people. Even one person.

I needed Cade.

And he did care about me. A lot. In his way. Where Henri had abandoned me, Cade had disobeyed a direct command to stay away from me.

That meant something. Even if he'd hidden things from me to do it.

Didn't it? Could we work this out? Did I want to?

Yes, I did. I loved him.

But we still had a problem.

After a long stretch of silence, I said, "I thought I could trust you."

"You can."

"That's what your words say. Your actions are saying something else."

"If I tell you everything I know, will it fix this?"

I turned and studied him. The tension in his posture, the tightness of his mouth, the small tic in his left little finger.

"It'd be a start." I couldn't promise more than that, even if I did love him. Not when I was still hurting about the whole Goddess-burned situation and how much it was looking like his good intentions would screw me.

Chapter 8: Cade

Cade had forgotten during his long, solitary years how much it hurt when you hurt the one you loved. Not that he'd loved anyone in centuries. Morris had done such a number on him that his first connection after gaining his freedom had been a twisted and dangerous thing that was all blood-soaked destruction. He hadn't been willing or able to let anyone close since. It'd been too dangerous. He'd used people to get his needs met—more gently than most *moroi* would, given he hadn't completely lost empathy—but he'd never let anyone in like he had Lya.

He'd done the right thing. The Darkwatch being here told him that. He could have handled her temper. But the hurt? Seeing her standing there, her proud anger not quite hiding the defensive hunch in her shoulders or the uncertain flick of her eyes away from his, as though she didn't quite trust he wouldn't glamour her, broke his heart.

Conscious of both the size and the magical strength difference between them, he slowly sat back on the bed and leaned back on his hands, spread wide so she could see them, his whole front exposed. Everything in him screamed not to do it, not to make himself vulnerable, not after the things Morris had done to him. But it was a risk he had to take. If she wanted to fight, he could take her. But if she ran now, those Darkwatch elves would be after her, and then he'd have to kill someone. He'd been down that road before. It didn't end well for anyone.

Her shoulders eased, but her face stayed hard, as if relaxing it would be some kind of defeat.

"First, I'm sorry," he said.

That earned him a heartbeat of meeting his gaze before she continued studying his chin.

"I should have told you. I didn't because I genuinely wanted you to have plausible deniability." He hesitated then told more of the truth. "And because I was afraid that if I did, you'd do something that'd get you hurt again. Lya…"

She met his eyes again, maybe hearing the genuine pain in his voice.

"That's why I followed you up here. That, I'm not sorry for. I'm sorry for lying by omission. I'm sorry it looks like I trusted Alejandro before you. I'm sorry you found out under the circumstances you did. But I'm not sorry for being here."

"To save my ass." Bitterness tainted her scent, almost palpably acrid.

It was all Cade could do to stay seated and not shake her. Damn the woman. Couldn't she see how much it meant that he'd let her into his defenses like this? That he *needed* her this much?

"No," he said. "To stand at your side. Like the partners we are." Then he hesitated. "Aren't we?"

A tremor ran through her like a dam on the verge of breaking. She started to answer then shut her mouth again and looked away.

That cut Cade deeper than knowing he'd hurt her. *Paving your own fresh road to hell with your good intentions. Hekate damn it.*

He kept his mouth shut, giving her space, even as he wanted to get up and grab her. The lump in his throat and the heaviness in his chest helped. He couldn't lose her, but she wasn't a pet in any sense of the word.

Had he been treating her like one? Easy blood and sex without the respect?

It'd been his pattern for every connection up to now. Respect for boundaries, yes. But otherwise? It was an exchange, and his past partners weren't enough to risk his own safety to allow them to mean anything to him.

With Lya though, the fact that he was asking himself about this now, in these circumstances, meant this conversation was long overdue. Especially given how she'd been treated by everyone before him and likely everyone around her, given she had one foot in Otherside and one in the human world.

Words bubbled up as he realized how she must feel right now.

Still, he waited. Kept his eyes on her feet so she wouldn't feel like he was staring her down. Tried to keep his breathing even, despite his heart pounding like he was in danger and preparing to fight, and the dizziness that accompanied the blood high he was on.

Two quiet steps brought her closer to him, and he barely managed not to jump when her hand rested on his chest.

"Your heart's beating," she murmured, sounding surprised. "What are you afraid of?"

"That I've fucked up the best thing I've ever had with the best person I've met in almost five hundred years." He swallowed the rest of it—that she'd leave him—not wanting to manipulate her into staying if life as whatever she thought she was to him didn't appeal to her anymore. That would backfire with her.

"I mean, you have."

Cade looked up before he could catch himself, afraid of what he'd see on her face, given the careful emptiness of her tone.

Her hand shifted to brush a stray lock of hair off his face. "But I'm not going to punish you for owning it."

A shuddering exhale fled him as he slumped.

Lya climbed on the bed, kneeling with a leg to either side of him, and draped herself over his back, wrapping her arms loosely around his chest. Her warmth soaked into him, even over that of the blood he'd had. "Don't get me wrong, I'm still furious with you. But I—somehow, I trust what you're telling me. You didn't lie outright. You just didn't tell me everything. It made shit harder for me. But I don't think you meant it to, and I'm really trying to give you the benefit of the doubt."

He tried to twist to look at her, but she tightened her embrace to keep him where he was. "I didn't, truly." He gently laid a hand on one of her arms and, when she didn't pull away, added, "Lya, I've been alone for most of the time since I fled Morris. I don't know what to do with these *feelings* for you, and after two hundred years of burying everything and then two hundred ninety-six more of keeping almost everyone at a distance, I'm trying to figure out what to *do* when I just want to keep you all to myself. It's not an excuse. It's just..." He didn't know what it was.

"It just is."

"Yes." Relief that she understood made him squeeze her arm.

She pressed closer against him but said nothing.

Again, he waited.

The kiss she planted between his shoulder blades made him jump in surprise. "I forgive you. But I need to know what you know about this before I get myself killed from ignorance."

"Anything. Everything." He tried twisting again, and she didn't try to stop him this time, making a surprised noise when he bore her down to the mattress beneath him and stole a rough kiss. "I'm sorry. I haven't been doing right by you. That changes now."

Her answer was to catch his face between her hands and study him.

"Thank you," she said before pulling him down for a kiss.

"Stay with me tonight," he said when they broke for air, not caring if he sounded demanding.

This time there was no hesitation from her, and she relaxed as though she'd been hoping he'd ask. "Okay." Her expression turned wicked. "But you'd better make it worth my while."

"I'll do my utmost best." He suited actions to words, rising up to pull off first his shirt then hers and her little shorts.

The bikini she wore underneath reminded him of what he realized he now thought of as home: their little bungalow surrounded by its overgrown yard in St. Augustine. Lya had once slipped into her native French while drunk on the beach and joked, "Vivons d'amour et d'eau douce, mais sans l'eau douce," not realizing he spoke the language as well.

Living on love and lack of fresh water, indeed.

As long as he had her, he'd make do. And he'd do what he could to make being with him feel like home, since she'd been driven from everything else that might be it for her.

For now, he focused on the bare brown skin beneath his lips and fingers. Her warmth and the faint crackle of magic, her little gasps as he pushed her bikini up to suckle a taut nipple and tease the curve of her breast with his fangs.

Lya arched against him until he gripped her throat and pinned her down with a snarl. He wasn't letting her go anywhere. She was *his*, and he'd almost lost her, again.

She gasped, pupils dilating as her body heat rose and her pulse raced. The scent of her arousal seduced him. Independent as she was, she *wanted* this. Wanted the force of his desire and his aggression in displaying it. She always had, even knowing what he was and what could happen to her if they went too far.

That trust was the biggest aphrodisiac he'd ever encountered.

He obliged her, locking gazes with her as he slipped his free hand between them and pressed into her slick warmth with two fingers. The little cry of pleasure she made, the needy moans as he curled his fingers within her, made him want to take her, but she'd come first.

When she shuddered around him, he rolled her onto her front to pull the strings of her top free. Then the bottom, throwing them both aside before leaning forward.

"This has excellent possibilities." He enjoyed the goosebumps his breath raised on her neck. Her body always responded to him, every little thing, and with the throbbing of his cock, he needed more. "Stay put."

Of course she didn't listen, shifting to her side when he stood to get his trousers off. He didn't mind though, given the appreciative eye she swept over him.

Still, he swatted her ass. "I said, stay put."

The saucy little minx grinned. "Make me."

That sent his blood pounding through him in a scalding wash. He took her at her word, drinking in the startled cry she made when he pinned her belly down with vampiric speed, swallowing it in a kiss.

Guiding himself into her felt like coming home all over again. His body covering hers, dominating her, pushing into her warmth, catching her cries in his hand over her mouth. She was so alive. So vibrant. And so very much his as she pushed back against him and spread her knees to welcome him in.

Cade barely held out long enough for her to come again then followed her, driving deep as he climaxed. He stayed where he was, kissing the sweat drenching her spine and enjoying the salt taste of her.

She shivered, from the cool air hitting her as they separated or pleasure or both, and Cade started to pull away.

Lya caught his arm. "Stay. I missed having you in me."

Happy to oblige her, he got an arm under her hips and shifted them both to their sides. As he brushed damp hair from her face, he checked, as he always did, that he hadn't left a scratch, fang mark, or bruise on her. Bad enough he'd given her cause to doubt his actions earlier.

Satisfied she was both unharmed and satiated, he curled closer around her, tucking his face against the back of her neck where the beguiling, blended scent of herby elf and earthy human was strongest.

Her sudden giggle snapped him out of the doze he'd started slipping into.

"What's so funny?"

"That Sequoyah bastard has no idea he contributed to my getting thoroughly well-fucked." She burst into giggles again.

In spite of himself, Cade snorted a laugh. "I hope you're not inclined to find him and thank him. Although if you did, he might give me an excuse to bite him again."

Lya laughed harder, and the broken piece of Cade's heart healed a little. She was as quick to anger as she was slow to forgive, but he might have found the balance. Either way, he'd take this moment and catalog it alongside the few other nice ones he had in his memories—most of them with her.

He tightened his arms around her and spoke before he could think about what was coming out of his mouth. "You're the light of my life. I would do anything to keep having nights like this."

Her laughter cut off but only because she twisted slightly to look at him then brush a kiss over his lips. "I never get tired of hearing that." A strange expression crossed her face. "Now go get me a towel."

"How about a whole shower?"

"Even better."

Cade carried her in, and by the time they'd finished fucking a second time and washing up properly, the entire suite was steamy and every surface fogged or damp. He cracked one of the windows looking over the beach, leaving the curtains open so he wouldn't forget while she finger-combed her curls and grumbled about not having any of her various hair products.

He caught her around the waist and gently pulled her back toward the bed. "We have planning to do, love."

Lya put her hair up in a bun before throwing herself onto the mattress and kept her voice as quiet as he had. "Mami Wata really told you something?"

"Mmm." Despite the humidity, Cade went back and shut the windows. He didn't know what shapes Alejandro could take these days but wouldn't put it past him to sit under the window. He shut the blinds and then the curtains before returning to where Lya lounged on the bed and lying down alongside her.

"There's a ritual that might appease the sirens."

"Might?"

"Mami Wata said it had to be done precisely. I wasn't sure what we'd do for blood, but with Darkwatch elves in town—"

"Are you serious?" she hissed. "You want to harvest blood from the Darkwatch to appease sirens in a spell you don't even know will work? Cade, that's *treason* for me to be involved."

He started to ask why she cared, given how they'd treated her, then held his tongue and took a minute to think about it. Cade had no idea what it meant for her to exist half in Otherside and half outside of it or how much more dangerous it would be for her if she went along with his plan. All he knew was he wanted blood for what'd been done to her and he didn't much care who paid it.

That's not your place. He grimaced and took her hand to kiss it. "We'll do as you think best, love."

She tilted her head back against the pillow and crossed her arms, less in anger than in instinctive self-defense. "There's no other way?"

"There's always another way, but all of them involve blood. Alejandro's a blood witch, so he could probably come up with something, but that means using a human. It's not like sirens accept chicken. Or horse, given we're more likely to find one of those here." He paused, debating whether to say the next thing, then steeled himself and pressed on. She'd wanted honesty. "Then of course, there's hoping the Darkwatch don't get clever and try using yours."

Her gaze snapped to his. "Shit."

"Yeah."

Lya pondered then frowned. "Not yours?"

"Oh no, mine will be needed to open the chest. But I'm undead. Sirens prefer the living." He drew a finger along the line of her throat. "Especially those who are in some way as liminal as they are, living halfway between land and sea, at least according to Mami Wata."

"Liminal. Like me," she whispered. "Halfway into Otherside."

"Precisely."

"That's the other reason Callista sent me. She probably ordered the Conclave to send the Darkwatch as well. She doesn't trust me after Morris, and she's too wily to let the queens get the drop on a treasure like this."

"Yes. Particularly given that a few of the things in it would be dangerous in elven hands. My guess is you were right. You aren't meant to come out of this alive. How better for Callista to please both the Lyon and Chapel Hill Conclaves while increasing her own power?"

She scowled. "The treasure is dangerous. Dangerous how?"

"Soul magic."

Her eyes flew open, and her jaw dropped before she recovered herself. "Soul magic? Are you shitting me? So even if I had recovered everything, I'd be guilty of breaking the Détente by transporting *soul gems* across the state?" She punched him in the chest, hard. "Cade! You should have fucking told me this!"

"I wanted you to have plausible deniability." He grimaced and rubbed his chest. She was strong for being only half-Otherside. "To be honest, I was also hoping I'd be able to beat you to it and buy out the debt. It really would be the easiest way to settle everything."

"It's just not the way Callista wants it done because apparently I'm too much of a pain in the ass. But *why?* What does she get out of this? Is it pure spite? Is it Farand again?" She pushed herself from the bed to pace, muttering imprecations under her breath.

Cade tried to focus, but her agitation and movement were increasing the scent of her in the close, humid room and making him salivate. He shifted to loosen the growing tightness of his boxer briefs. "Lya."

She ignored him and kept pacing.

"Lydia." The sharper tone and her full name caught her attention.

"What?" she snapped. "I have a right to be—oh." She stayed where she was for a second, breathing deep to calm herself down, and went to reopen a window after peering out and making sure there was nobody outside before coming back to bed. "Sorry."

When she returned, he couldn't resist grabbing her and holding her close, both to wallow in her scent and the warmth of her body and to reassure himself with all this talk of people who wanted her dead. He'd come too close to watching her die once already, and he didn't want it to happen again.

Lya snuggled closer. "We'll figure something out."

He knew they would. He just didn't like any of their options because he couldn't shake the conclusion that, one way or another, the woman he loved was going to get hurt. Badly.

Chapter 9: Lya

I had a dilemma to resolve.

Cade was right. There was no way this mission didn't end in blood, one way or another. It wasn't that I was a stranger to it—a few of my hunts in London had resulted in an Othersider leaking. Where I had a problem now was in how clear it seemed it was my blood intended to be spilled.

I was a huntress, not prey, no matter what anybody thought about the half-human in Otherside.

So as the sun rose, I lay in Cade's bed, his arms tight around me, as though even in his sleep he was afraid I'd leave him. That shamed me a little, that someone I loved would be so afraid of me leaving.

But at the same time, it wasn't all on me to own. Yeah, some of it stemmed from my issues. But some of it was all his. We'd work it out, or we wouldn't. I loved him even more than I'd loved Henri. At the same time, I'd learned the hard way I had to look after myself.

It wasn't just looking after myself though. I had something good with Cade, and he'd already made some questionable decisions here. I knew desperation when I saw it, and he was just about there when it came to doing what it took to keep me with him. Hell, I'd forgiven him last night because I recognized the impulse in myself: to protect the one I loved at all costs.

All costs. That swirled in my mind.

What would I do to complete this mission without damning Cade to Torsten's dubious mercy? Even I knew a master vampire would destroy a younger one who'd killed his own sire. I'd killed Morris in the end, but Cade had made a solid start of it.

Yeah, I needed to do something about what I'd learned last night. Unfortunately, the only people I could leverage were Mami Wata—who clearly wasn't having it, regardless of what favors Cade might have purchased—or Alejandro.

I choked down bile at the memory of how he'd eyed me.

It wasn't just sex he wanted from me. It was everything. Sex, blood, life, soul. I'd seen the look before, in the kelpie I'd brought in once. Even without Cade's warning, I'd known the witch was dangerous.

Desperate times called for desperate measures.

Fine. I'd approach Alejandro and see if I could pull this off.

Decided or not, I hesitated. I didn't like this plan. I'd been warned not to let Alejandro get me alone and I didn't want to leave Cade. He was, unusually, still warm even after two vigorous fucks and with the sun rising. I'd gotten used to his coolness, even enjoyed it in the Florida heat. But there was something nice about having him warm, his heart beating faster than usual, even if it was still too slow for anyone alive.

Stop it.

He was what he was. I loved him for it, and all of this was stalling based on novelty. I pulled away—or tried to. His arms tightened, and he grunted a negative.

"Cade. Babe." I leaned over and kissed his temple.

"Mm?"

Not quite awake then. "I need to go eat something."

With a huffed sigh, he let me go, still not fully awake. I stood at the side of the bed drinking in the sight of him, praying I wasn't making a mistake, then got dressed in yesterday's slightly damp clothes and grabbed my gear. After paying for another day's parking for my car on the mobile phone app, I grabbed the room keys, shouldered my rucksack, and left Cade's suite as quietly as I could.

The sound of my knock on Alejandro's door seemed too loud in the dawn silence, and I winced, hoping it hadn't been enough to wake Cade. He'd be more alert with the blood he'd taken. Maybe enough to wake up. Guilt squirmed through me as I tried to tell myself this wasn't the same thing he'd done to piss me off. This was still my mission. I just needed to figure out what the hell Alejandro's angle was, and that wasn't going to happen with Cade standing guard.

I had my hand raised to knock again when the door swung open.

"Oh," I said before I could stop myself. "Ugh."

Alejandro, clothed only in an open robe that left his entire front bare, grinned sleepily, completely unabashed as his willy greeted me enthusiastically. "To what do I owe this singular pleasure?"

"Breakfast. Now."

His gaze flicked past me to the empty hallway, and his eyes narrowed. "Just us?"

"For now."

The leering smile returned. "How intriguing. A moment, bonita."

Rolling my eyes, I nodded and crossed my arms to lean against the wall next to his door. A few minutes later, the door opened again. He was properly dressed this time, in a tight cotton V-neck tee, linen trousers, and leather sandals, his long dark hair slicked back almost the same way Cade's usually was. He'd fit right in with the more well-to-do tourists, even with the macabre collection of talons and bones on their leather thongs.

I gritted my teeth and headed for the stairs without a word. He was almost as quiet as an elf as he followed me, even as we hurried down. I kept a careful space between us as we waited for a table, which seemed to amuse him more than anything. When we were seated and I had a heaped plate from the continental breakfast buffet, he rested his elbows on the table and held his coffee up to his nose.

"Swill," he sighed, "But it is difficult to get the real stuff this far from the source."

I didn't reply, focusing on getting at least a few bites into me to stall the conversation.

"Come now, bonita, you have to tell me what this is about sooner or later."

"I'm not bonita."

He grinned. "You are but very well. What should I call you then?"

"L—"

The way his attention sharpened, and he leaned forward ever so slightly gave me pause. I remembered Cade had never said my name in front of him.

"Lady," I finished lamely. "You can call me lady."

Disappointment flashed in his gaze. Then he smiled. "Very well. So?"

"What's your endgame?"

He didn't look at all surprised by my bluntness. "The treasure, of course. Has Cade told you what's in it?"

"Yes."

Setting his coffee down, he leaned back in his chair and spread his arms. "So you must understand why I want a piece of it."

Of course. Cade had said Alejandro would have become a lich if he could find a djinni or other means to break the Détente and do it. He must be after the soul gems in the haul. The gold and whatever else wouldn't hurt, but the soul gems would be primary.

"That's it?" I asked.

His gaze lingered a little too long and a little too intimately on the place where the now-healed bite marks had been on my neck. "I admit, you offer a certain fascination for me. Could I convince you to—"

"No." I glared. "I'm Cade's." It was still strange to say the words, but when messing around with beings more than ten times one's senior, one didn't get hung up on shit like feminism or personal autonomy.

I was independent, not stupid. Well. Not *that* stupid.

Alejandro inclined his head. "Very well. Now that we've cleared all that up, I'll ask again why you wanted this ungodly early meeting without your lord's presence."

"You remember we talked about the sire—" I glanced around the quiet restaurant and lowered my voice anyway. "The singers?"

"Yes. Pesky things."

I frowned. He spoke about them like they were common pests, not unusual and deadly dangerous. "How would you get rid of them?"

"Other than giving them you?" He grinned as I stiffened, the look carrying equal parts amusement and dangerous intelligence. "Come now, lady, I've lived too long not to see patterns. Callista has so very many resources at her disposal, and she calls upon *you.*"

Offended, I opened my mouth to snarl at him then flushed with a wrathful blend of annoyance and shame. He wasn't wrong. From what I'd gathered, Callista was one of the most powerful Othersiders on the US East Coast.

Alejandro seemed familiar with her, and he didn't even live in the territory. He chuckled. "Don't take it poorly. You have your charms. They just happen to be perfectly used as bait in this situation."

"Fine. So what's your plan? Because I know you have one. Living as long as you have? You wouldn't risk facing Cade and me together."

"Too true, sadly."

A server approached with the ham and cheese omelet he'd ordered, and we both fell silent until he'd topped up Alejandro's coffee and gone away.

"My plan was to either separate you two or use a mundane." He grinned and shoved a bite of eggy mess into his mouth at my glare. "But with the shadows here? My dear lady, we'd be fools not to use them, since I'm assuming you're not volunteering."

I ate a few bites of my own food, annoyed that his plan and Cade's were effectively the same. Maybe it was a five-century club thing.

"Don't tell me you're averse to the idea?" he said.

I shrugged. "I have my reservations."

Reservations like still holding out hope that, one day, my exile would end and I could see my homeland again. I didn't even know why I wanted to. Everyone there had thrown me away. There was nothing for me in Lyon or London anymore, and everything for me if I stayed here with Cade. But some part of me wanted at least the *option* to return. If I was judged an elven traitor, that couldn't happen. Ever. Door closed. Maybe it needed to be. But I wasn't ready for that yet.

We nearly finished our meals before Alejandro spoke again. "You're softer than I expected, for such a hard little huntress." He smirked. "All the more fun to break."

I snarled, holding my knife in such a way that I could easily stab him over the table if I needed to. "Don't you even dare think about it."

"How could I not? Such a mystery deserves to be…well, not solved in this case." His eyes roved over me again, coldly avaricious, and I shivered. "Let's say carefully taken apart, piece by piece."

Everything I'd eaten sat heavy for a moment as my stomach and my brain warred in the decision of whether it would come back up. Blessedly, my brain won, but it was a near thing, and I swallowed hard. "If you touch me—"

"Yes, yes. Don't worry. Cade's already given me the talk. Very bloody. Still. He might not always be here." His expression turned thoughtful. "How lucky for you that the singers prefer shadows to drinkers."

I couldn't help my shudder. I'd known Alejandro was a dangerous ally at best and a temporarily amicable knife in the back at worst, but this was well beyond what I was comfortable with.

Time to wrap it up.

"That's it then?" I said. "Your plan is the shadows?"

Amused delight sparked in his eyes as he nodded and finished his omelet.

"Fine. Enjoy the coffee." I rose, leaving some of my food and most of my own coffee.

At the way he focused on what I was about to leave on the table, I piled it all up, brushed the table off, and took the dishes with me, depositing them amid the few other plates and cups in a bin atop a cart next to the kitchen. Who knew what a witch like Alejandro could do with saliva, hair, or whatever else he might glean from my leftovers? I wasn't going to make it easy on him. The frustration painting his face when I glanced back told me I'd been right.

"Bastard," I muttered.

That'd been horrid. I wanted a shower, but I needed to make a quick stop at the variety store again. I'd planned on a day trip yesterday, not an overnight, and while Cade might not mind "earthy" smells, I needed deodorant and toothpaste, maybe a new T-shirt as well. I could have just headed back to my own hotel on Hatteras Island, but that would have meant delays I didn't have time for. And if I was honest with myself, I didn't want Cade thinking I was running. I owed him that much.

Callista texted while I was waiting to check out, and I couldn't help jittering. The cashier frowned a little as she rang everything up but didn't say anything. I was just another tourist girl, and she probably thought we were all odd.

I checked the message when I was outside.

Well?

She wasn't keen on helping, I sent back. *I'm working on an alternative plan.*

I assume that means Cade.

My heart hammered, and adrenaline spiked. Of course she knew. He'd shown himself to the Darkwatch. They answered to the queens, not Callista, but they had no reason to hide last night's run-in from her.

Her next text made my stomach sink. *Nothing to say? I know he's there.*

Sweat broke out down my spine as I wavered. This needed a phone call. I started walking to the marina at Silver Lake and dialed.

She picked up immediately. "What did I say, girl?"

"I know. I'm sorry. I—"

"You nothing. The queens are screeching over last night's business."

"What was I supposed to do? Brennan Sequoyah was trying to beat the shit out of me for no damn good reason!" I hissed. "Was that what you sent them here to do? To beat your errand girl senseless?"

Silence. I couldn't tell whether it was fury or because I'd accused her of sending the Darkwatch and she'd hoped I wouldn't see that. When she spoke, her tone said it was maybe both. "I meant what I said. Torsten is my next call."

"Callista, no, please." I hated myself for begging, but we had to pass through a wide swath of North Carolina and all of South Carolina to get home. If Torsten wanted to make an issue out of Morris's death and set an example for his coterie without actually harming any of his own people, Cade would be the perfect tool.

Bonus for Callista—it'd hurt me too, which seemed to be the object of all of this. Punishment for defying her, killing Morris, and running off with Cade.

Her voice became venomously sweet. "What would you be willing to do?"

Suddenly, the breeze off the water was too cold. I stopped where I was, seeing the new layer to what was going on. She'd known Cade would follow me or at the very least hedged on it. That had to be why the Darkwatch were here. Cade and I had wiggled out of her last job for me. She wouldn't accept a second failure or the way it undercut her authority. She ruled the Carolinas with an iron fist, and putting her reputation in the dirt was the only reason she really needed to make my life difficult.

I suddenly wondered how much of a coincidence it was for Alejandro to turn up at Cade's the day after she'd contacted me. The old Othersiders, those who lived over a couple of centuries, tended to know each other, even if only by reputation. Callista's was big. Big enough I wouldn't bet against Alejandro knowing of her and keeping tabs on what she might be interested in.

"Well, girl? I'm waiting."

What would I do for Cade? My heart clenched.

"Anything." The whispered word caught in my throat, but I knew she heard it.

Chapter 10: Cade

Cade woke to cold sheets and an empty room at sunset. Lya had gone, returned, and gone again, judging by the new plastic bags on the dresser. He was debating whether to call her when the lock turned and she blew in, stopping short when she saw him rising from a defensive stance.

"Oh, hey. You're up." She came to him quickly enough that he wondered if he'd imagined the brittleness of her smile, but the way she hugged him tight chased away his worries.

"Hello, love." He kissed her hair, holding her close as he breathed in the scents she'd brought with her. Sun, water—marina, not beach—fried food, beer. Spent the day in research at a bar then. "Good day?"

"Um. I guess." She leaned back, and her face twisted. "Alejandro's a piece of work."

He snarled to show fangs. "What did he do?"

"Don't worry. Nothing you need to have a go at him for." She slipped free and shrugged her bag from her shoulders before setting it next to the dresser. "He agrees with you though. About using the Darkwatch as bait."

Cade forced himself to pause and be still long enough to chase away the specters of what the blood witch might have done to her before saying, "Lya, Alejandro is dangerous. Stay away from him if I'm not there. I mean it."

"Yeah." She shuddered. "Don't worry. I won't be repeating the experience anytime soon if I can help it."

He nodded, not quite satisfied but trying to be as she messed around with the bags on the dresser, pulling things out and transferring them either to her bag or the bathroom. Nothing that needed to be done urgently and yet all things he would have expected her to do earlier. Something was off. "Everything okay? It's been a while since you were up in the day."

"Callista's day shift." Something flickered in her gaze then, and her scent soured in fear. "I hate that bitch," she added softly.

"We all do. What did she do this time?"

"Had me chasing around town trying to find something to appease Mami Wata."

He grimaced. "How'd that go?"

"It didn't." She paused in her movements to hug herself as she looked at the floor. "I need a Plan C. She's getting impatient. Pushed me to use you."

Aha. That's probably it. He reached for her, rubbing his hands along her arms. "That's why I'm here, remember? I'm at your service, love."

She relaxed and went on her toes to kiss him, a light brush of her lips that he savored. "I know. I love you. More than I can say. I just hope I can show you."

Cade stole another kiss before going back to the bed to sprawl on it in a way he hoped would distract her from her agitation with Callista. Sure enough, her eyes drank in his nakedness as he said, "I took care of Mami Wata anyway. There's nothing to smooth with her. She knows you're with me."

"Try telling that to Callista." She stepped closer to the bed and drew a finger over his body, a small, pleased smile replacing her earlier frown. "But thanks. I'm not exactly a natural ambassador. I'd rather just stab things."

"Speaking of stabbing things, love, if we're not going to use the Darkwatch, we need another option."

Lya flinched and grimaced, shaken out of her admirations. "We can use the Darkwatch."

"What?" He sat upright against the headboard as she shrugged and joined him. "I thought you said—"

"I know. But I've been thinking all day. Why am I acting like there's a place for me at home? Home." She scoffed bitterly. "Home is where people love you. Where they stand by you and choose to be with you." Her brown eyes rose to his. "Home is with you now. I could be the perfect angel, and they'd never let me back. So fine. Fuck them and fuck trying to be the model exile. Treason it is."

"Oh, Lya." His unbeating heart twisted for her pain, even as, shamefully, relief and joy suffused him at her choice. He'd suspected, just based on a few things she'd said in the last few months, that she'd been holding out hope to return to Europe someday. Why, he couldn't figure out, but she'd wanted it, so it was what it was. Coming to terms with that no longer being an option, and that she had to be the one to shut the door on it, was a lesson he'd learned after being turned but hadn't wanted to push on her. He still remembered how much it hurt though.

Cade opened his arms, and she threw herself against him, hiding her face against his chest.

"It's okay, love," he said. "Let it out. It's hard to be here, feeling like you can never see loved ones again."

A spasm shook her then another, as she tried to keep holding everything in. To his surprise, she didn't pull away and go for a walk like she usually did.

He stroked her hair. "You're no less strong for feeling everything you're feeling. You're strong for seeing a hard truth and making a difficult choice."

Another quiver. Then the damp warmth of tears prickled on his chest alongside an aborted sob. He slouched lower on the bed then lifted her legs over his so he could cradle her better. This was why she'd stayed awake and away all day; it had to be. They'd both gotten used to being solitary, and while he'd found himself craving the presence of others, she had an unusual loner streak for one of the usually social elf-blooded. Maybe it was something natural to her, or maybe it'd become her armor when she'd been first treated differently and then cast out. Either way, he'd learned to let her flee when she was troubled, even if it was clear it hurt her more than anyone to be alone.

This was the first time she'd come to him with the fallout. He hated it, and yet it gave him hope they could grow together.

When she wound down, she shifted so she could scrub her face. "Sorry."

"Don't be."

"Can you promise me something?"

"Anything, love."

"Whatever happens with this job, don't let Callista or Torsten have you."

Cade frowned. "Why would they—"

"Just promise me, okay?"

His grip on her tightened before he caught himself. If it'd keep her safe, he'd absolutely give himself over.

"Cade. I mean it. You have at least another couple hundred years before the risk of mental decay starts, right?"

"Yes. More if I keep getting Otherside blood, but—"

"No, but nothing." She curled tight against him again. "I never had that long, so don't throw it away over me. No matter what happens."

He didn't like this talk. It sounded like she was already planning for something to happen. Actively planning, not just worrying or coming up with worst-case scenarios. He wanted to dig into where this was coming from, but if he did, it would only push her away again.

"Fine," he said. "You have my word."

Lya finally relaxed all the way. "Thank you."

Cade let her be for a few minutes longer, content to hold her and tease himself with her warmth and the pulse of blood moving through her. Yesterday's feasting had thoroughly sated him. He'd never had half-elf, water spirit, and high-blood elf in the space of twenty-four hours before. While he'd happily drink from Lya or even a human just for the taste and enjoyment of it, he was mindful of her needing to keep up her strength and his needing to stay as unobtrusive as possible.

Pounding on the door interrupted the moment, and Cade winced as Lya jumped and jostled his sensitive parts. She was up and heading for what he assumed was a weapon in her bag.

Alejandro's voice called, "Cade? I know you're up."

Sighing, Cade rose and pulled on yesterday's trousers before getting the door. "We're up."

The witch lit up at the "we."

"Remember our agreement," Cade snarled as he opened the door wider.

With a smile that was too sharp to be charming, Alejandro slunk in. The look became more genuinely amused when he spotted Lya pretending to examine one of her tantos while sitting at the room's small table. "Feisty, isn't she? Delightful."

"I like 'prepared' better. Especially with the Darkwatch and other trouble in town." Lya narrowed her eyes at Alejandro. The way her gaze traveled over him made it clear who she considered the other trouble to be, which reassured Cade somewhat.

Completely unfazed, Alejandro clapped. "Just so. In our chat this morning, the lady here was coming around to the idea of using the Darkwatch elves as bait. Is that correct?"

She nodded, more a jerk of her head. "I accept that the other options are more distasteful."

"Agreed," Cade added.

"Perfect. Then I have a proposal."

"A proposal." Cade gave the witch a steady look with more than a hint of threat in it. "Need I remind you what happened the last time you made a proposal?"

Alejandro flicked a hand dismissively. "That was then. This is now."

"I fail to see what's changed."

"Everything. For now."

Lya eyed them with a blend of annoyance and curiosity, so Cade shrugged and said, "Fine."

"We use her as bait."

Cade's blood surged, and his heart lurched into beating. "No. Absolutely not. We all know—"

"Hang on," Lya said. "I smelled Aether all damn day, so I know the Darkwatch elves are following me. It's not exactly a big town, so even with me trying to shake them, they have to know I'm here, at this hotel. Let's hear the rest of it, and then *I'll* decide."

Alejandro's smug look was insufferable, but Cade ground his teeth and kept his mouth shut.

"As I was saying. We know the Darkwatch are watching the lady. They know you're here, Cade, because you're a chivalrous fool. But they may not know I'm here or what I am."

Lya frowned. "I draw them out. Cade is the obvious decoy. You're the hunter."

"Literally." Alejandro extended a hand, and with a ripple, it became canine, reverting back when her eyes widened. "We only need one elf, but more gives us room for error."

Cade closed his eyes in a long blink before nodding. "It gets the job done. I agree on getting more than one if we can." Lya wore the stubborn look she got when she didn't want to do something and was going to do it anyway, and Cade bit back the question of whether she was sure she was okay with committing treason. Instead, he asked, "When?"

Lya stood. "It has to be tonight. Now, even. Callista is out of patience. Besides, the sooner we get this done, the sooner we can go home. The ferry back to Hatteras runs until midnight, so if we can get it all done by then, so much the better."

Alejandro eyed her, considering, but only made a small bow. "As the lady commands."

"Good," she said. "Cade, where do we need to go for the negotiation or spell or whatever? And what will we need other than blood?"

"Just the blood in the water—or better yet, flesh—and the incantation I got last night. They range throughout the sound and through to the ocean shallows offshore, but it should be easy enough to summon them to shore."

"Got it. If we head to the north, we can lure the elves with a pattern change and be closer to the ferry for when we're done."

Cade nodded. "It's also lightly wooded to the north, so between the trees and the dunes we should have enough cover in addition to the darkness. Fine. I ride with you. Alejandro follows and sets up an ambush."

"Pack your bags and bring them," Lya said. "It'll look like we're going to leave town. That'll get their attention."

Alejandro slanted a look at her. "Just don't think you're leaving town without me getting my share of the treasure."

"You'll get what you're owed, mate. Don't worry." Lya's toothy smile suggested that might or might not be the treasure.

But Alejandro just smiled. "In that case, I'll excuse myself to prepare. Shall we reconvene in half an hour?"

Cade shrugged. "Works for me."

"Me too," she said.

After the witch was gone, Cade gathered her into his arms. "You okay?"

She wilted a little and blew a breath out. "He's kind of a lot, and it's been a long day. But if we can get this done tonight, we can go."

There was something unspoken at the end of her sentence, like she'd wanted to say "home" but couldn't bring herself to.

"Are you sure everything is okay?" he asked.

"It will be." Her grim tone, and the small scowl pinching her brow said she was determined.

But again, he got the sense it was something more than just this job, and he couldn't quite convince himself it was just about the prospect of committing treason. "Love, don't do anything foolish, okay?"

Lya gave him a small smile and went on tiptoes to kiss him. When he clasped her hips to pull her closer, she wrapped her arms around his neck and molded her body against his. When her tongue darted into his mouth, it snagged a fang, and the burst of herby, sweet blood made him stiffen and try to pull away. But she held him in place.

A gift, then. She was too experienced with him by now to have done that by accident, and if she wasn't pulling away it'd been intentional.

A low groan of pleasure slipped from him, and he slid his hands from her hips to the crease of her ass to lift her. She wrapped her legs around his waist, pressing closer and squeezing as though she was trying to meld them together.

"I love you. More than anyone, ever," she said when she pulled away. "I know I'm… I have bad habits, and I run from you sometimes instead of using my words. But I hope you know I always love you."

"And I you." He kissed her once more before reluctantly letting her down so he could pack his things and she could ready her weapons.

As they left though, Cade realized she hadn't actually promised him she wouldn't do something foolish.

Chapter 11: Lya

My agreement with Callista weighed on me as we headed to the northern end of Ocracoke Island. Cade's attempt to get me to promise not to do anything foolish weighed heavier. He knew something was up. He was too clever not to, and he knew me too well. The combination of a predator's observation skills combined with his own loving attentiveness meant I couldn't hide shit from him. I could deflect or run but not hide.

Hopefully, he'd forgive me or at least see I'd made my promises out of love for him.

I chattered the whole drive to keep him from digging further. "Will Alejandro be pissed if you come back to Hatteras with me after?"

"Not if he gets what he wants, although he might get greedy at the end." Cade glanced at the rearview mirror again, where a big, black SUV, the hybrid kind favored by the Darkwatch, trailed us. A few other cars were going our way, one of them also being Alejandro's surprisingly unremarkable Nissan Altima—red, of course—and I hoped the rest were heading for the ferry rather than the beach pull-off I'd spotted on my way down here.

"Greedy how?" I asked.

He shrugged. "Trying to take more than the thirty percent cut he agreed on. Or somebody's blood, bone, or pelt. Something I haven't seen coming because he's probably picked up new tricks in the century and a half it's been since I last worked with him."

"You think he will?"

"Absolutely. I'm counting on it. He has his own sense of honor, but he is completely aligned with the tricksters."

"Counting on it as in, you have a backup plan for betrayal, or as in, you hope he does it so you can exercise those protective instincts you keep curtailing?"

He turned to me and stared. "I hadn't realized I was being that obvious about it."

Grinning, I said, "A little."

"Sorry." He winced.

"Don't be. Do you know how many people have ever cared enough to want to protect me? Zero. Other than you, of course." I reached for his hand and squeezed. "It'll be okay. How long is the ritual supposed to take?"

"Shouldn't be long." He kissed my hand. "A few words to gain the siren's attention, some blood in the water, a few more words, and we should have a siren or two."

"Are we talking the winged sort or the fishy sort?"

"Mami Wata didn't say. She's far from home, so I imagine the shoal she keeps an eye on is as well. Might even be a mix, although I've never seen a blended shoal. They tend to stick to like."

As so much of Otherside did. The Triangle's power sharing agreement was the only thing odder than my mixed-species relationship with Cade, except that agreement was based on mastery and predation rather than our love and equality. Most of us were just too territorial, especially given the shrinking space for us as the human world grew exponentially and our slower reproduction rate and more niche needs had us gradually decreasing. We were coming to a pinch point, but that was above my paygrade to deal with.

Then I caught on to something. "Wait, does that mean you've encountered sirens before?"

He nodded, his expression darkening. "I'm glad you thought to get earplugs. The last time Morris's crew ran into a shoal, I only survived going overboard because I was already dead and there was living blood in the water."

"Oh. Shit." A chill ran over me. "I wouldn't have thought the undead could be affected."

"Sirens might not want undead blood, but their song doesn't discriminate between the living and the dead. They call to those with longing." He sighed. "I've always been afflicted with a great deal of it, one way or another."

That didn't surprise me. As far as I'd seen, two kinds of vampires survived the first few centuries: the depraved who learned to leash their instincts well enough not to get caught and those who were still so painfully connected to their humanity that it was a wonder they survived. I wasn't a fool; I knew Cade was content with his lot as an undead and had made peace with what he was and had to do to keep living. But he was definitely one of the latter, for all he saw himself as a shark and occasionally acted like one.

"We're here," I murmured, spotting the turnoff and pulling in to park. There was just enough space for a few vehicles, and I smiled grimly as I wondered what the Darkwatch was going to do. I hadn't lied when I'd said I'd smelled them around all day. I just hadn't mentioned that the reason was because Callista had told the Luna in the triad to meet me to discuss the terms of the agreement she'd extracted from me in exchange for Cade's safety.

The Darkwatch SUV slowed just enough for me to see a frustrated face in the passenger window then kept going. Alejandro followed.

I smiled grimly at the multiple layers of deception going on. The Darkwatch had to pretend they weren't following us. Alejandro had to pretend he wasn't with us. I had to pretend I had no idea that the Darkwatch had picked up our tail so quickly not because they'd been watching but because I'd told them I'd be going along with Cade and Alejandro's plan—to get blood in the water and lure the sirens in, not that it was supposed to be their blood. I swallowed bile as my stomach twisted.

This could all go very terribly wrong, but I'd made the Luna show me Callista's text ordering them to spare Cade. It had to be worth it.

"Everything okay, love?" Cade asked.

"Yeah." I got out before he could press and went around to the trunk where my kit was stowed. I was already geared up— Beretta nine-mil on one hip, Walther PPK in waist holster under my shirt, CUB knife in its sheath on my left forearm, a silver-edged tanto sheathed at my back, and earplugs in my pocket— but I needed to grab the Sawback for Cade. It was a risk carrying a damn machete on the beach, but it was full dark now, with the moon still close enough to new that humans would struggle to see in the dark. He could glamour the fuck out of anyone who did see anything, or I could do a minor mindmaze. Leaving the car might earn me a ticket or a tow, but I'd deal with that if I had to. It'd be fine.

As long as nothing went sideways.

"Let's go," Cade said as soon as he'd belted on the Sawback and secured the second strap around his thigh.

The wind coming off the Atlantic tried to rip his words away, but I heard him. We jogged over the dunes together. The spot we'd chosen on the Maps app was a little less than a mile up the beach and would pass the off-road vehicle path I assumed the Darkwatch would use to park. I would have used it myself, but driving a Ford Escape down a path meant for four-wheelers would have called too much attention to me—attention I'd rather have on the Darkwatch and Alejandro, if it came to it. It was obvious, as far as traps went, but Cade had agreed it'd make following us irresistible.

I tried not to let the feeling of exposure get to me as we jogged past it. The dunes and scrubby trees didn't seem high enough to hide us from what we'd be doing. The wind coming off the ocean would surely carry any shouting or screams. Otherside battles were nearly always silent, but I had no idea what to expect with sirens. The whole point was that they were loud enough to be heard by a ship's crew over crashing waves.

I couldn't shake the feeling that, one way or another, this was going to be even messier than we'd planned.

Less than ten minutes later, we'd reached a good spot. Or as good a spot as any. The beach was narrower and the trees a little thicker, with just enough curve of land that we wouldn't be in view for any ferries on the Hatteras-Ocracoke route. I didn't bother catching my breath before laying an Aetheric ward as far out as I could manage, reaching both the tree line and the waterline. It wouldn't keep anyone out, but it'd let me know if someone was coming.

As I finished, a red wolf trotted out of the trees and stopped, a chunk of flesh between his teeth. I held completely still until it shifted to become a naked Alejandro.

He spat the bloody hunk into his hand and licked his lips. "Lady. Cade."

The blood in human-like teeth was even more disturbing than it had been on a wolf, and I shuddered. Cade was much neater with his meals.

"Where's the Darkwatch?" I asked.

"Tending to the one I hamstrung down the beach." His smile widened as he passed the gory spell bait to Cade. "They were looking for you two, not a wolf."

"Please tell me it was the Sequoyah."

"If that was the blond one, then yes."

I relaxed a little. Each triad of Houses in a Conclave had a different specialty with Aether. In North Carolina, the Monteagues—like my mother's House—could manipulate the minds of others. The Lunas could manipulate auras, and the Sequoyahs were healers. The catch was, unlike djinn, we couldn't work magic on ourselves. With the physical healer of their trio out of commission, the other two would have to stabilize him by mundane means before completing their mission. We'd still have our hands full with one or two elves, but the odds were better.

"Are you staying like that?" Cade asked him.

"For now," Alejandro said. "Hard to speak a spell otherwise."

"Fine. Get back to the tree line. We'll give it another few minutes to draw the elves closer." Cade wrinkled his nose at the chunk in his palm. "This should be enough to start, but they'll want more."

Alejandro shrugged and made his leisurely way back to the wind-twisted trees.

"Where do you want me?" I asked.

"Not near the water. The fishy type are fast even on land—think alligator or charging bull sea lion. They look slow, but their upper bodies are powerful enough to make a good pace." Cade toed off his shoes then took off his socks with his free hand, tucking them inside before handing both to me. "The flying type could come out of nowhere, although my bet is we'll be dealing with the fishy ones. There aren't enough rocks here for perching."

"Fast and beefy. Got it." I backed above the tide line then looked at how high the waves were crashing, remembered the tide was coming in, and backed up even farther before putting Cade's shoes behind me.

When I was far enough back, Cade bowed his head, looking like he was offering a prayer or making a wish. Then he waded into the ocean, heedless of getting his trousers wet, and began the spell.

I gaped. Cade had said, "a few words," but this was a song so full of beauty and power I could barely stand it, carried on a baritone so full of longing I wanted to cry. I hadn't even known he could sing. He'd been a pirate a long time ago, so yeah, sea shanties maybe, but this was…incredible. The words in an unknown language crawled over me, stinging my soul and pulling everything I'd ever wanted to the forefront of my heart.

An itch of paranoia pulled me away and warned me I had Alejandro's attention. I could just make out the witch in the dark but knew he was watching me, not Cade, and all at once I remembered what Cade had said about the possibility of betrayal.

Glaring, I stuck my earplugs in.

This was the dangerous part. Not only did we potentially have sirens coming from the sea, but we also had elves in the mix. And of course, Alejandro himself.

Cade must have finished the song because he knelt in the water, unbothered by how it splashed over him, and when he stood again, the chunk of flesh was gone.

Nothing happened.

I frowned, scanning the beach while staying angled to keep Alejandro in my peripheral vision. I didn't dare remove my earplugs.

Just as I was getting anxious, something triggered the ward on the beach side. I spun back, forcing my hand away from my weapons. We were guests here. Violating the peace before we'd even introduced ourselves would ruin everything.

Spotting the siren made it that little bit harder to stay cordial.

I'd gotten the sense that Mami Wata was far more than she appeared. The siren took no such pains to disguise her appearance. Behind long dreads adorned with shells and gold rings, eyes as dark and flat as a shark's peered from a medium-brown humanoid face with gill-like nostrils. Long, serrated teeth showed when she smiled up at Cade, cunning and anticipatory. She was gorgeous but clearly not human and just as obviously deadly, with a bare upper body that could rival a wrestler's and a heavy lower body ending in a long tail like a dolphin's. Somehow that was the surprising part, after all the human representations showing them as more literally fish-like.

Her lips moved, and Cade swayed, shaking his head like he was trying to clear it before gesturing back up the beach the way we'd come. As she turned to follow his gesture, her gaze fell on me. Her chin lifted, and her gill-nostrils fluttered—and then she lunged, moving like a sea lion but much faster.

I scrambled backward.

Cade, moving with the vampiric speed only the well-fed old ones could manage, was in front of me in the blink of an eye. He shook his head at the siren and pointed again down the beach.

She leaned to look around him then glanced back up, answering with a sly smile.

He stiffened, his gestures growing more aggressive as the siren's did. I couldn't tell whether it was posturing or real concern.

Movement in my peripheral vision made me whirl.

Alejandro was emerging from the trees, head cocked in wonder and avarice. The siren's hungry look twisted to anger as she too saw him, and at the same time, my wards flared farther down the beach.

Shit was about to hit the fan, and we had more players incoming.

Chapter 12: Lya

I clenched my hands into fists to stop myself from reaching for a weapon. I couldn't bloody hear anything, which meant I didn't know how close we were to breaking the truce. Laying a hand on Cade's shoulder, I said, "Someone else is coming."

From the way the siren's angry expression pinched tighter to fury, with nostrils flared and teeth fully bared, they weren't her sisters.

The Darkwatch had finally made it.

The problem was the siren didn't want more elf meat. She didn't want Cade, despite all his longing, and she didn't want the novelty of Alejandro.

She wanted me.

Her mouth stretched wide, and a single note poured out loud enough that I could hear it even through the earplugs. I clapped my hands over my ears, trying to keep it out, but it wasn't a seduction. It was a summoning.

The waves boiled higher as more sirens burst forth. The two elves ran straight into them, stopping hard and backpedaling for the woods. A red wolf cut them off, snarling and slavering.

Hands shoved me, and I stumbled back. Cade. His mouth formed the words "go" and "run" as the first siren gripped his legs with clawed hands and pulled him down. Even as I watched, her mouth moved, and he stopped fighting to rise as a silly smile curled over his face. The elves wavered then dropped, likewise affected. I hadn't told them there'd be sirens involved, just that the treasure was hidden somewhere here, and they didn't have earplugs. Only wolfy Alejandro and I were unaffected.

I should have gone. We'd lost control of the situation. Even if the sirens would accept a meal of elf in exchange for the treasure, they'd want something from me as well. I stood frozen, staring at Cade, heart thundering.

I couldn't go.

I couldn't stay.

But I couldn't leave him.

Callista's voice echoed through my thoughts. *What would you be willing to do?*

And my answer: anything.

I already owed too much. I was twice indebted to Callista now, once for the cost of my exile and again for Cade's trespass. Part of me was bitterly resentful about it—her putting me in the situation, him not listening to me. But as the siren cocked her head and narrowed her eyes, trying to figure out why I was still standing and not either fleeing or on the ground with the rest of them, I decided it was time to stop running.

I could owe a little more, set aside the self-preservation that'd driven me to take the bounty on Cade that'd resulted in this whole mess, if it freed someone I loved.

"Stop," I whispered. Then I shouted it. "Stop! If you stop singing and talk, I'll—I'll make a bargain."

She grinned then turned to call to her sisters. The wolf, now hovering nervously at the tree line, made no sign that I could interpret. He just stood there, head low, watching the sirens like a real wolf would watch a herd of deer for a weak or vulnerable target.

With a deep, shaking breath, I pulled out the earplugs.

"Ah," the siren said in a voice like the wind in a shell. "Clever girl. What bargain?"

"What did Cade promise already?" I gestured to him when she looked confused.

"More flesh. Those." She tilted her head to the downed elves. "We desire you, being between worlds."

I eyed her sisters as they moved closer. "We need the treasure."

"Which?"

"The one Mami Wata entrusted to you. A chest, one only he can open." I pointed at Cade.

"Mm." She grimaced. "That presents complications."

I took a breath and let it out slowly to stop myself from shouting at her. "What complications?"

"Many wish to acquire this chest. Him. You. Those. A djinni. More."

"What are they offering?"

Another sharp grin. "Nothing like you."

I answered before I could talk myself out of it. "Free Cade from the spell and bring us the chest. Then you can take the elves for your trouble and some of my blood."

Her features tightened, a little greed, a little frustration. "Blood only?"

"Blood only. Look, we're taking this chest off your hands. Nobody can get into it but him, so it frees you from the obligation Mami Wata laid on you to guard it. Right?"

"Correct," she agreed grudgingly.

"So?"

She looked again at her sisters and spoke in a language that sounded like a blend of dolphin chitters and gull cries, punctuated by the sound a wave made slapping against a rock. It wasn't the language Cade had spoken. It sounded more like something that'd work at sea.

Turning back to me, she said, "Deal. But! You wake the undead one yourself, if you can."

My stomach plummeted. "What?"

She shifted her body up and down in a shrug. "The old ones come back. Sometimes. Often not. Find something he longs for more than the peace he is offered now. The deal offered is shadow flesh and dusk walker blood, the deal accepted is the chest of treasure Mami Wata entrusted to us. More is out of balance. Do you accept?"

I wanted to say no. I wanted to demand she bring Cade back. But I was out of options.

"I accept," I whispered.

The siren chittered to her sisters again. They made their way back to the waves, re-emerging with hooks attached to thick ropes. I swallowed, hard, as the still-living elves were speared through the shoulders and dragged into the ocean like sides of beef.

"Wait here," she said.

I didn't trust her sly smile. Sirens were technically part of the fae faction in Otherside, and I had a feeling I'd just made a bad bargain. That'd be deadly if I didn't figure out how she'd twist it by the time she came back. I didn't trust Alejandro either, now shifted back to human form and crouching off to the side. Odds were good there'd be a double betrayal.

First though—Cade.

I knelt and pulled his head into my lap. He was damp with seawater and encrusted with sand, still smiling as though whatever picture the siren had painted behind his closed eyes with her song was the most entrancing and beautiful thing he'd ever seen. Blood might be enough to draw him out. I sure as hell couldn't sing, and I didn't know what else I could offer. Words but I wasn't any good with those either.

The same frustration that'd overcome me in his hotel room earlier washed over me now. Why hadn't he just fucking listened to me and stayed away? Now he was trapped in some dream, and I was trapped as much by my oath to Callista as I was on this damn beach with a shapeshifting blood witch and a siren due any minute now. I didn't dare offer Cade blood yet. If the siren tried to screw me out of the deal, I'd need my full strength.

A splash announced her reappearance and that of her sisters. A fourth had joined them, and with an effort, they dragged a square chest roughly the length of my forearm on each side between them.

"Come for it, dusk walker," the bargainer called.

After a moment of hesitation, I did.

"Your blood," she demanded.

I slowly drew the tanto from its back sheathe, but before I could cut the bend of my elbow, she lunged and tackled me. My surprised gasp earned me a lungful of seawater as a wave crashed over us. I was choking and drowning as a tug on my ankle pulled me deeper. Claws bit into my leg, and from the sting of the water, I was bleeding. I scrabbled, but there was nothing to grab in the tan sand of the beach. Another clawed hand swiped at my right arm.

You never specified how *the blood would be given or how much*, echoed a voice in my head. Not mine, something pushed on me by the grip around my ankle, still pulling.

I kicked with my free foot, and it connected. The iron grasp on my leg disappeared as an outraged scream echoed in my head. I managed to break the surface of the water and haul myself back up the beach to take a hacking breath of air.

A sound like a gull's warning cry pulled my attention.

Alejandro had charged the beach with the Sawback that'd been strapped to Cade's thigh. He darted in, naked and shifter-fast, and lopped the tail fluke off the nearest siren, who was trying to drag the chest back into the water as well.

I clapped my hands over my ears at her piercing cry of agony, which cut off as suddenly as it began when he swung the blade across her throat. The other three sirens snarled as they abandoned me and the chest and faced Alejandro.

"You got what you wanted. Go," he said.

"Murderer!"

"Betrayer!"

As usual, the witch was completely unaffected. He smiled.

"Go now, or we can try again. Your songs won't work on me." He dabbed a finger in the dark fluid oozing slowly from the body at his feet and rubbed it between that finger and his thumb before licking it. "And I have blood now. Would you like to see what I can do with it?"

"Give us her body."

"No. You tried your trick and failed. You knew what the price would be. Fetch it later." The cruel curl of his mouth said what his words didn't: *what's left of it.*

With an impotent howl of rage that had me flinching again, the sirens retreated and vanished under the waves.

I clutched my gashed arm to me and limped out of the water, grimacing at the combination of salt sting and fabric abrasion. "Why did you save me?"

"Lucky accident for you. Frankly, you weren't my concern."

Of course I wasn't. My lip twisted in a sneer. "What now?"

"Cade and I had a deal." Alejandro smirked, looking me up and down. "But deals can only be enforced when both parties are alive and able."

This was too much. A deal gone sideways not once but twice, my blood in the water, my knife lost, Cade effectively dead-dead, and to top it all off, I'd participated in treason when I'd let the Darkwatch elves be dragged under the waves. "What the fuck do you want from me then, you honorless jackass?"

"Everything. Eventually. But I'm feeling generous tonight, and this harvest is far more valuable than a half-elf. How about this? You let me walk away with the treasure. I don't kill you both here and now."

Panic flared in me. I had to get the treasure back to Callista, or my life—and now Cade's as well—was forfeit. She wouldn't accept just the other favor she'd wrenched from me, not when it was the gems she wanted. I was fucked six ways from Sunday.

Then a twinge at the base of my skull reminded me of the tracking tag I'd put on him.

I pulled on Aether and stood aggressively, hoping he'd take it for posturing rather than subterfuge as I swiftly refreshed the tracker.

"Fuck you!" I shouted.

"We could. You must be a good lay to keep a vampire's attention this long." His cock stirred even as his hand shifted, sprouting the tan fur and wicked claws of a puma. "I don't think you'd enjoy my version of a happy ending though, sweet lady. Take option one. Back off and enjoy what time Cade has left or put him out of his misery. But if you stay here or follow me, it's option two. I kill him, have my way with you, and kill you while I'm at it."

I pulled harder on Aether, like I was thinking of attacking, then let it go and stepped away from him.

"Fine. Take it." I didn't have to fake the bitterness in my voice then. I might choose to fight another day, but I wanted more than anything to put this fucker down here and now. Like the sirens, though, I had no interest in seeing what he could do with fresh blood as powerful as a siren's would be, and I had to try to save Cade. Besides, I hadn't completely failed—the elves didn't have the gem, and I was more than capable of tracking Alejandro down.

"Smart wench. Get your master and go."

I gritted my teeth against the reflexive protest that Cade wasn't my master. What I was to him didn't matter. Getting him out of this mess did. I trudged back up the beach, not looking forward to hauling Cade's dead weight out of here on my injured leg before any humans came to investigate what they might have heard out here.

"Before you go…" Alejandro approached, Sawback in hand.

I stood over Cade's still prone body. "Don't even think about it. If you're such a good blood witch, figure it out yourself."

He narrowed his eyes at me. "Fine. But I'm keeping this." He whirled the machete.

"Whatever. Just stay the fuck away from us and don't harm either of us in any way. Deal?"

"Deal."

I didn't trust him to keep to it, but he had a treasure and a cooling siren's corpse to play with. I'd trust that—as he'd said—those were more interesting for the moment than me and Cade.

With an effort, I lifted Cade and maneuvered him over my shoulders in a fireman's carry. He was bigger than me, both in height and weight, but if I could at least get the shorter distance to the ORV trail where the injured Darkwatch elf would be waiting for his fellows, I could carjack him or something and drive us back to my car.

Alejandro didn't follow as I focused on putting one foot in front of the other in the sliding sand. My torn arm and ankle throbbed, and the wind pushed at me like an insistent child. I prayed I wasn't leaving enough blood in the sand for Alejandro to use then figured if he could use it, he would have by now. Maybe the salt in the ocean water was corrupting it, although that didn't seem to stop him from wanting the siren.

I'd gotten maybe a thousand feet when I stumbled and lay where I'd fallen, heaving.

This wasn't going to work. Cade was too heavy, and I was too injured and tired after donating to Cade, driving several hundred miles in a handful of days, and getting much less sleep than I usually did. I'd have to fetch a car and come back for him.

I managed to drag him into a patch of dune grass and prayed the wind would carry his scent inland and not toward Alejandro. Who the hell knew what the witch might use vampire blood for beyond opening the chest, especially with Cade alive but unresponsive. I thought about giving him some blood and trying to revive him there, but then I'd be even more fucked and he'd probably need more than was safe to give him now. The scent of my wounds hadn't stirred him, so I didn't dare do more now.

Car it was.

The black SUV from earlier was parked exactly where I'd thought it would be, at the end of the ORV trail. Brennan, the elf who'd sucker-punched me, was seated on the bumper. The white fabric of a bandage made a wide band around his right thigh, and he peered into the dark in my direction with his gun at the ready as I crouched behind a dune. He must have scented me or heard my labored breathing, but he hadn't spotted me yet.

As quickly as I could, I pulled on Aether and formed a sting that I sent at him in a burst of magic. "Be still!"

He staggered, dropping his gun and falling to one knee with a sharp cry of pain.

I wasn't strong enough to put him out completely, but it'd take him a minute to fight off the mental compulsion and fight back—a minute I wasn't going to give him.

I burst over the dune and ran at him, bashing him in the skull with the butt of my Beretta so he'd go all the way out. I wanted to kill him, but I could still technically argue I hadn't killed the other two elves and therefore was only guilty of misinformation and accessory to death, which might get me out of a full treason charge. Killing Brennan outright would definitely get me charged with treason if one of my cousins could do a truth read or a Thread of Thorns interrogation at trial. I couldn't risk it.

Digging in Brennan's pockets, I found the car keys and got in. Turned the big vehicle on and pulled around the body on the ground to drive as quickly as I dared back to the spot on the beach where I'd left Cade.

He was still there.

Practically sobbing in relief and exhaustion, I dragged him into the SUV's back seat, turned around, and got us back to my car. Wherever Alejandro had parked, it wasn't down this access. Either that or there was a spell at work. Regardless, I couldn't see it, and I cursed the missed opportunity to disable his car.

I pulled up alongside mine and moved Cade to my backseat, in an echo of this past summer, and then covered him with a tarp, tucking it carefully over him. We had to get back to Hatteras tonight, and there was no way in hell I was going to explain an undead man to the people on the ferry.

With silent frustration, I hurled the Darkwatch SUV's keys as far as I could toward the ocean, cut all the tires, and bandaged myself up before getting us on the road to the ferry. My plan was to get us at least back to my hotel.

And from there, I had no idea.

All I knew was I had potentially just lost everything in one fell swoop, and I'd be damned if the fuckers who'd stolen it from me got away with it.

Chapter 13: Cade

The first, last, and only time Cade had been glamoured was when Morris had lulled him to his death, the one kindness his sire had ever offered him and that more to ensure he went quietly. He remembered the spiraling plunge into euphoria, the pleasure of the bite even if he hadn't known what it was, followed by the sensation of being weightlessly, effortlessly alive…until he wasn't.

Falling prey to the siren's song had felt something like that, except rather than the high of euphoria, there was a mellowing, a surcease of anguish. He had everything he ever wanted.

Mentally, at least.

Lya smiled at him in the moonlight. "What are you waiting for, babe? Let's go!"

He had no idea where they were going, but all he wanted was to be with her. He'd follow her anywhere. And he did, passing long decades in a dream until a richly blended scent of earth and herbs and woman reached him.

Lya's blood.

He stopped following her. She wasn't bleeding in the dream.

She turned to him again. "What are you waiting for?"

It came to him like the snap of a broken bone. This wasn't right. This was very, very wrong. He shook his head. "No. No, this isn't real."

"Of course it is." She pouted. "As real as you want it to be anyway. Isn't this what you want most?" Her hands slid up and over his chest as she went up on her toes to kiss him.

It almost worked. Almost.

But as his hands skimmed over her, he found her wearing the sort of low-cut bodice gown women had worn in his original time…nearly five hundred years ago. Well before Lya could possibly have existed.

The dissonance clanged through him.

"This isn't right," he whispered. The scent of blood came again, stronger, alongside the salt scent of both the sea and Lya's sweat, despite the moonlit field he saw. She wasn't here with him. She was elsewhere and hurt and struggling.

The siren's song.

Memory hit him like a slap. He'd summoned the siren, with the words Mami Wata had given him. Simple enough, even if it'd been ages since he'd spoken ancient Greek. He'd tried offering her the elves, but she hadn't wanted them.

She'd wanted Lya, and she'd sung him to his second death to get her.

The last of his contentment slid into sick horror as he realized he'd be aware when the sirens started eating him, assuming they didn't spit out his undead flesh and simply drag him under to drown.

But he wasn't drowning. No water was filling his lungs. If anything, it felt like he was floating, or…being carried? Then a jolt. He was flat again, and the dream started again.

He followed Lya under the moonlight.

More decades passed, until again the rich scent of her blood came when she wasn't bleeding in front of him, only this time it was on his tongue. Then filling his mouth. Then he was choking on it as someone massaged his throat.

This. I want this. I want her, the real her, not this phantom. Let me go. LET ME GO!

The dream shattered, and the gasping inhale he drew had him aspirating blood. He coughed as Lya swore and jerkily lifted him to a propped-up seated position against the warmth of her body.

"Sorry," she muttered from behind him, pounding his back until he stopped choking. "Come on, come back."

Her voice was stronger than the siren's. He gripped the arm in front of his face and bit down hard, his instincts telling him to use his fangs to secure the hold on the flesh. At his back, Lya jerked and made a strangled-sounding whimper, but if he focused on easing up he'd lose the thread that was holding him here.

"Fuck, that hurts without a glamour. I hope that means you're coming back. Please come back."

Keep talking, love. Be my anchor.

"You're probably going to be furious when you find out what happened, but please just come back. I'd rather you be mad at me than…than trapped."

A little more, love.

Another whimper as he pulled on the vein. She clutched him tighter with her free arm and the thighs he was sitting between. "Please come back. I promise I'll tell you everything. I won't run, even if you get mad at me."

The last thread binding him to his undead life tightened, and with a groan, he withdrew his fangs. "Lya."

"Cade! Thank the Goddess."

With an effort, he worked enough saliva into his mouth that he could heal his bite, frowning to find damage not just from his fangs but from what looked like the clean slice of a knife and the more ragged slashes of a clawed hand.

"Oh, love, what happened?" he rasped when he'd coated all of it in at least a little healing saliva. "Are you all right?" Then odd scents reached him. Old, stale room, marshy land, not the sea. "Where are we?"

"Squatting in an empty house somewhere between Nag's Head and Plymouth."

The place names meant little to him, but only one thing mattered. "You're safe?"

"We are, for the moment, until someone finds the car and comes to investigate. I wasn't going to make it all the way back to the Triangle tonight though, and we couldn't stay in the Outer Banks."

He wanted to look at her, but the effects of the siren's song still lay heavy on him. "The treasure?"

"Gone. Alejandro took it after killing a siren when they tried to grab me and take back the treasure. Gave me the option to walk with your body and nothing else, or he'd use me as he pleased and kill both of us. I chose option one."

Fury gave Cade the strength to pull away from her, although he fell heavily back on his elbows when he tried to turn and see her. "What?"

Guilt and outrage tightened her face in the faint greenish light from a glowstick. "He said your deal with him was only enforceable if you were able to enforce it. I could go, and take you with me, but only because the treasure and a dead siren were more interesting."

Cade gaped at her. Not because he was surprised by Alejandro but because self-preservation topped her list of priorities. Carrying him out would have threatened that, but here he was.

She really did love him.

He hadn't realized a seed of doubt had been germinating in his heart after her reaction to discovering him in town the other night, making him think that maybe, if pushed, she'd leave him behind, given he wasn't supposed to be here anyway.

Lya looked off to the side, answering the question he hadn't dared to ask. "I wasn't going to run. I couldn't leave you. Even if—"

"If what?"

She avoided his gaze, focusing instead on her leg, which was also bandaged. "I owe Callista twice now. Once for the treasure. Once for you."

"Me? What the—"

"She knew you were in North Carolina. The Darkwatch told her. She said her next call was Torsten and that she was going to tell him you killed Morris. I couldn't let her, Cade. I'm done with just looking out for myself."

Suddenly too exhausted to stay upright, Cade slumped to the floor. Dust swirled, almost as much as his thoughts. Of course. He was so used to being alone or dealing only with a local coterie that it hadn't even occurred to him that the Darkwatch agents might tell Callista.

"What did it cost?" he asked as neutrally as possible.

"She still wants the treasure." Her gaze flicked to him, then away. "But I was also supposed to go with the Darkwatch after we'd delivered it."

"*What?* Why?" Suddenly, the reason for her insistence that he not let Callista or Torsten have him became clear, and he leveled a knowing look at her.

Lya flinched. "I don't know. But I told them where we'd be, and then I told you where we should go and agreed with you we should kill them but didn't tell them we'd be summoning sirens." She pulled her knees up and buried her face against them. "I made an utter mess of everything, and now we have no treasure, two Darkwatch agents eaten by sirens, me guilty of several crimes against the Chapel Hill Conclave, and—"

Cade pushed up enough that he could touch her. "And our lives. We'll figure this out."

How, he didn't know. This was as fine a fuckery as he'd ever found himself in. He wanted to be angry with her for the double—triple?—cross and for letting Alejandro escape with the treasure that should have bought her freedom. The damned witch might be the only person on this coast who could circumvent the spell on the chest, given enough time.

But she'd given up the treasure and the price of her freedom from Callista to save his life. Twice.

Everything in her expression and posture radiated misery. "At least I was able to refresh the tracking tag on Alejandro."

"You were? Clever. We might have a chance to salvage this."

"I really hope so." Her eyes darted as she searched his face. "How mad are you?"

With a sigh, he pushed himself to sit beside her against the bare wall and lifted an arm. "Come here." After a brief hesitation, she slid against him, and he curled his arm around her before kissing the top of her head. "I'm disappointed that you didn't tell me what was happening with Callista, but I also have no room to be because I came up here behind your back to begin with. Alejandro is my fault as well."

She relaxed against him, easing closer. She smelled of dried blood, musty seawater, and fear-tinged sweat, but he'd take this over the siren's dream any night.

"We both thought we were doing what was best," she whispered. "Sorry it didn't work out that way."

"Me too."

They sat in silence for long enough he thought Lya might be falling asleep. She probably needed it, badly, having been up all of the previous night, most of the last day, and most of this night as well, with attacks on her throughout. He needed some rest too. If it hadn't been for feeding so well this week, he would have needed far more of Lya's blood to come back. As it was, a full day's rest and some human blood wouldn't go amiss. But they were in dangerous territory, and both of them would be hunted if they didn't get that treasure back.

As he was trying to think how to frame it, Lya shook herself. "Can't rest yet."

"I know. We both need it, but…"

"Yeah. Alejandro is still somewhere directly east of us, which means the treasure is still somewhere in the Outer Banks. Not on Ocracoke anymore but behind us."

"How accurate is the tracking tag?"

She scratched the base of her skull and grimaced. "Not at all this far away. It's meant for short-range tracking—people in the same city. Right now all I know is east, not even how far. Where would he go to work on the spell?"

Cade frowned. "My first response is 'home,' but I don't know how many other hidey-holes he might have established in the last century and some. He always was a creature of habit though, and Florida was his favorite place in the New World. Something about all the magic and misery in the soil."

"Ick." Lya shivered. "Okay, so if we assume he's going to make a run back to Florida, he's going to need to pass us here to get to 95 South. What are the other options?"

"Anything in the realm of possibility?"

"Yes."

He lifted the hand not holding her and counted. "He takes the treasure to Callista himself and negotiates a deal, probably throwing me into the mix to get it open faster and safer. He takes however long it takes to reverse engineer the spell on the chest and opens it himself. He finds somewhere new to stash it until he can kill us, which gets him my blood to open the chest and ensures we won't come after him." Cade grimaced. "I suppose there's always the djinni as well."

"Djinni? What djinni?"

"The last job we did together, we found a bottle. Blue, with an eight-pointed star painted on the base in silver. I opened it, and a djinni popped out. Nearly killed the both of us before acknowledging the debt."

Lya twisted to look at his face. "Did you get wishes?"

"Of course." He chuckled. "Alejandro was furious when I didn't share, but I'd found and opened the bottle. Besides, he'd been a pissant the entire job. Nearly got me killed. I suppose that's why he put a silver knife in my back in the end. Lucky for me one of my wishes was resistance to it."

"You're resistant to silver?"

"Not really, not anymore. The effect started fading decades ago, after I lost the talisman."

His other two wishes—the location of another of Morris's caches and the name of a human who would safely turn gold and gems into modern funds with no questions asked—had been well spent. He could have figured them out on his own eventually, but that'd been what he'd wanted most at the time. The safety and security his master had stolen from him, bought with Morris's own treasure.

"Did you get the djinni's true name?" she asked.

"Yes, I think it amused him to give me that so he could have an opportunity to kill me later. Summoning djinn is dangerous, Lya."

"And having a blood witch, Callista, the Darkwatch, and the Master of Raleigh after us isn't?"

She had a point. Still, djinn were tricky creatures. They never gave anything for free, and the giving of his true name meant Nebuchadnezzar would expect something in return for its use. But Cade kept coming back to the fact that they were in a race against time, needing to recover the full treasure before Alejandro could open the chest. He had no doubt that, when the witch discovered the soul gems in the cache, he'd take those. So would the djinni, if he discovered them, and that would be just as dangerous. Since that was likely what Callista wanted as well, their options were short. It'd be better for Nebuchadnezzar to have the gem than Callista because djinn laid much longer plans. Cade would have time to work something out, either to recover it or to prepare for the eventual fallout.

"Fine. What do you want to bargain for?" he asked.

"Can he just bring us the treasure, now that we've recovered it?"

"Likely yes." Cade considered that. "If all we asked was for it to be brought here, that shouldn't cost too much. Shouldn't. He wasn't a fan of Alejandro, and he knows Ale is a blood witch. That'll drive the price up. Then again, it gives the djinni the chance to kill the fucker."

"Sounds win-win?"

"Maybe. It's never that easy with djinn."

"What are we willing to lose?"

"For my part? Everything but you."

"Same. So who cares if it's easy? We're already completely fucked."

She was right, but the caution that'd kept Cade alive this long still weighed on him. "Fine. But you wait outside while I summon him so you don't hear his true name. That'll take some of the leverage away from him. Leave your knife, with a little blood on the edge, please."

She did as he asked, hissing as she made another small cut in her forearm before handing him the knife. When she was gone, he scratched an eight-pointed star twice the length of his arm on the wood floor in the style he remembered from the bottom of the bottle, then jabbed the bloody knife in the center of it.

Stepping away, he said, "Nebuchadnezzar, I call to thee. As flames undying light the way, as heaven holds earth under its sway and all that lives comes to fall, let nothing bar your answer to my call. Come now, Nebuchadnezzar, and hear what I offer in trade."

Nothing happened at first, and Cade was just beginning to wonder if he needed more of Lya's blood when the pressure in the room dropped. At the center of the star, a cloud of fire and lightning, like that Cade had once seen over an erupting volcano, crackled into visibility. Eyes the shade of carnelians sparked above razor-sharp black teeth.

"Cade the vampire," the djinni said. "Already desperate enough to make another bargain?"

"Nebuchadnezzar. Thank you for coming."

"Well? I haven't got all night."

"A moment. It's not just me, and I didn't want our third party to hear your true name." He turned and called, "Come on in," loud enough that Lya would be able to hear him from outside.

Nebuchadnezzar scoffed and rolled his eyes as she entered the room. "It's bad enough I have to watch Callista's brat without dealing with more elven by-blows. Who the fuck is this one then?"

"I'm Lya," she said before Cade could. "What common name may I address you by?"

Nebuchadnezzar chuckled, showing sharp black teeth. "She's smarter than you were, vampire, and more courteous, to give her name first." He studied Lya for a few seconds, before coalescing into the form of a tall, lithe young man with umber-dark skin and laughing dravite eyes, dressed in an expensively tailored suit. "You may address me as Duke."

"Thank you, Duke."

Cade eyed her sideways, wondering where the hell a half-elf had learned to treat with djinn. Elves and djinn had been enemies for millennia.

As though answering his unspoken thought, Duke said, "It's the high-bloods I can't stand. Don't worry. I won't give your lady love a cursed object." At Cade's snarl, he added, "What? It's obvious. I can smell her blood in you, but she doesn't have the fawning look of a pet. Anyway." He flipped a hand and started rocking on his feet, never leaving the edge of the invisible circle defined by the points of the star. "Now that I'm here, what the hell do you want?"

Lya crossed her arms and lifted her chin. "To buy a favor."

The djinni smiled avariciously. "I'm listening."

"There's a treasure," she started.

"Oh, fuck me. The one Callista's been on about?"

Cade grimaced. "Likely yes."

"What's wrong with it? She sent—ah. She sent you after it." He pointed at Lya then at Cade. "And you fucked it up, which means I benefit from an opportunity. Lovely."

"It gets better," Cade said. "The blood witch from our last encounter has it now."

Duke chuckled. "Grimm will have my eyes if I don't call her in for this."

Chapter 14: Lya

I was running on fumes, but my mother had taught me about dealing with the djinn. The same open-mindedness that had led her to fall in love with my father had also inclined her more than most high-blood, royal elves to learn how to deal peaceably with the rest of Otherside. It just hadn't given her the courage to stand up for me. That was apparently asking too much.

She'd given me three rules. Never lose courtesy, no matter how much they vex you. Never accept gifts, no matter how much they tempt you. And never show weakness, no matter how close you are to your deathbed.

I didn't know who Grimm was, but I inclined my head. "Your colleague will be welcome at the negotiating table."

When I looked up again, Duke was eyeing me with a blend of amusement and consternation. "Where did you find this one, Cade?"

"Around," he replied in a slow drawl that said he wasn't giving the djinni shit.

"She's far better mannered than you ever were." The djinni turned to me again. "Tell me, little fish, who taught you courtesy?"

"Fish?"

He wrinkled his nose and eyed me distastefully. "You smell like you've been in the ocean."

"I have." I smiled with more strength than I felt. "Sirens are a bitch to fight off."

That caught his attention. "Oh?" He glanced at Cade again then back at me. "This might well be a tale worth hearing. Free me from the star and step outside. I'll call Grimm."

Cade looked like he was going to protest until I put a hand on his arm. We'd summoned the djinni. We had to play his game.

With a sigh, Cade said, "Be free in this place, so long as you harm no one here."

Duke shivered and stepped quickly to the side then waved for us to go outdoors. We went, walking until we were out of earshot. I slumped against a tree, giving myself a minute to be tired.

"Where *did* you learn to treat with the djinn?" Cade asked.

"My mum," I said, unable to keep the note of sadness out of my voice. I didn't know if it was because of the reminder that she hadn't fought for me or because I'd resigned myself to never seeing her again only yesterday, but a wave of melancholy crashed over me so hard my knees almost buckled.

"I'm sorry." He reached out to brush my cheek quickly with his thumb.

"It's fine. We all make our choices in life, right?"

Before he could answer, the screen door to the house slammed. I pulled myself together as Duke approached us with another djinni wearing the form of a slim, pale-skinned, red-headed woman with sullen blue eyes and a faint sneer.

"You must be Grimm," I said with the same courtesy I'd shown Duke.

"Another marshmallow?" She sniffed. "Faugh. Not even a real one. Duke—"

"Hear them out. I think you'll be intrigued," Duke said.

With an effort, I set aside the double insult of the slur and the dismissal. Cade seemed content for me to do the talking, so I did. "We're after Callista's treasure."

Her attention sharpened so suddenly I almost jumped. "You're the one she sent after it?"

I nodded.

"So where is it now?" she asked.

"In the hands of a blood witch," I said. "A very old one."

Grimm looked at her nails, pretending disinterest. "And?"

Cade tilted his head. "Do you know what Callista is after?"

Both djinn hesitated then shook their heads, looking irritated.

I phrased my offer carefully, given how badly I'd screwed up the one with the sirens. "If we tell you and you deem it worth your while, I would ask you to retrieve the chest, bring it here, and keep word and deed of this deal secret. No more, no less."

Grimm scoffed. "What could possibly be worth the trouble of a blood witch?"

Cade just tilted his head and smiled. I stood there with my heart pounding and my guts twisting, praying our last shot wasn't going to literally disappear into thin air.

Duke laid a hand on Grimm's arm. "I'll agree, if only to hear the story of how sirens were involved."

"Sirens?" Grimm perked up. "Is that why the halfling stinks of the sea? Fine. Agreed."

"There are soul gems in the cache," Cade said, his gaze as sharp on them as Grimm's had been on us.

"And Callista only wants the one," I added, teeth gritted at yet another insult.

Grimm's eyes flashed to ruby and shone with pure greed. "Is that so?"

The djinn looked at each other. Duke nodded first. "Tell us of the sirens and then where this witch is. We'll fetch the chest back. You will open it and give over anything we wish."

I cleared my throat. "No. Callista wants all the gems. Leave us those."

Sneering, Grimm said, "She'll get the gems we leave her. She's had more than enough of everything else."

"No," I said again, even though I agreed with her. I had to deliver.

"Then get this chest from the witch yourself." Grimm looked at her fingernails, which became talons even as we watched. I shuddered at the memory of the siren's claws, and she grinned. "Ah, that's right. You did meet some sirens."

"They had the chest," I said grudgingly. The story had been part of the deal. "They sang everyone to sleep but me and the witch. I made a bad deal, and they tried to take me and the chest both back under the sea."

Duke held up a hand. "*You* managed to resist them?" He glanced at Cade, eyes narrowed. "And pull one of the long undead out of a siren's song?"

I nodded.

"How?"

"That wasn't part of the deal. You only asked for the involvement of the sirens. I gave you that," I said. It was hard not to sound overly smug, given how easy an answer earplugs were. "Are we even now?"

Duke rolled his eyes. "Brat. You're just like the other one. Fine."

I didn't know what "other one" he was referring to, so all I said was, "He's to the east. Near Nags Head, maybe."

"You'll have to do better than that, little fish," Duke said as Grimm scoffed.

I thought back to the beach. "He'll have siren blood, bone, or flesh on him."

Grimm pursed her lips. "That will narrow it down considerably. Stay here."

Both djinn disappeared with a shimmer as they changed planes.

I dropped down to rest in the grass then popped right back up when I found it damp. I'd had more than enough of being wet in the last day.

"Everything okay?" Cade asked.

"I'm exhausted," I blurted then pressed my lips together. This mess was kind of my fault, and I didn't feel right complaining.

He reached and gathered me to his body, and I slumped gratefully against him.

"Lya," he said. "This might not be the time or the place, but I want to propose something."

Propose? I couldn't help tensing. "What's that?"

"I want to give you some status among the vampires. Just in case something does happen."

"Status?" I repeated. He was making me anxious with this.

Pulling away, he tipped my chin up. "You can say no, and nothing will change. But if you say yes, Torsten and his coterie can't touch you, even if they take me."

I swallowed, hard. "Are you asking me to marry you?"

"What? No. But I would ask you to let me declare you my solidaire."

My heart skipped. That was a big deal. Maybe almost as big a deal as a marriage would be, except that, duh, vampires didn't marry as a general rule. They definitely didn't marry food or blood pets. Nobody had ever offered me anything like this. I had no title in my mother's House, and Henri bloody well hadn't come close to offering me a damn thing beyond his dick.

Could I trust this?

"I've heard the term, but what does that mean for us? For me?" I asked.

"For us, nothing more than the usual. That you're effectively my heir as well as the executor of my daylight business or anything else that I can't do. In the old days, it meant you'd be a source of blood and bound to protect me during the day. All things you already do."

"Yeah, because I love you."

He smiled. "And I you. But I haven't raised it before now because, well…"

"Because I run."

"You do. Until today." Cade studied my face, brow pinched the way it was when he couldn't figure out what I was about to do. "Like I said, it means you'd inherit my wealth and property if Torsten did find out about Morris, and you could find safety among a coterie without trading blood for it if something happened to me. I could also gift blood back to you."

"Which you did once already," I pointed out. It'd saved my life, but it was largely forbidden for reasons I didn't quite understand.

"Yes." He cupped my cheek and caressed it with a thumb. "Don't tell anyone though, hey?"

I frowned. "Are there reasons other than the don't-turn-elves thing?"

"A swallow or two here and there won't turn you, but it will strengthen you. Maybe not quite to full-blood strength but more than low-blood. It'd lengthen your lifespan as well."

"Ah. The master vampires don't want random non-vamps running around who are stronger than they should be and immune from consequences?"

"Basically, yes. Don't give me an answer now. Think about it, okay? Think of any questions, let the concerns simmer. I won't lie, it is a big step. But you could have—*should* have—left me on the beach. You made a deal with Callista to keep me safe. I might not like the results, but you've been acting as a solidaire would, taking pains to protect me. This is the only thing I can offer to thank you."

"You don't have to thank me," I said, although my head was spinning at what he'd said. More power? Immunity from vampire trouble? I didn't think Cade needed to do anything to thank me, but I also wasn't going to turn down perks that came with a role I was already playing. At least, I didn't think I would.

Then again, he hadn't quite treated me like an equal partner of late. Would this just be more of the same? Was it really protection? Or was it some kind of leash to keep me from running again?

I nodded, accepting that I needed time to think about this, and he pulled me back to him for a kiss.

"Well isn't this cute," Grimm said.

I jumped as much for the surprise of her voice as the heavy thump on the ground that accompanied it, wondering what, if anything, she'd heard. The djinni smirked at me as Duke materialized alongside her.

"Your treasure," he said. "Open it and let us complete this bargain before Callista notices us missing."

Cade hesitated long enough to make the point that they weren't in charge before walking to them, biting into the meat of his hand and squeezing his fist to make heavy drops of blood splatter over the metal cross nailed into the top of the chest. Dark wood glistened under the sliver of moon. He murmured a few words, but I couldn't understand the ones I caught. They sounded like English and French smashed together with something else.

Duke tilted his head. "Middle English. I haven't heard that since the Crusades. Your master and the Viking were contemporaries?"

"Roughly. Torsten is the elder by a couple of centuries. Quiet." Cade switched back to Middle English and smeared blood on two more crosses as a prickle rose on the back of my neck. Magic was rising, strong enough that I could feel it even if it wasn't Aether. Vampires weren't supposed to be able to do magic, so what the hell was this?

From the looks of consternation on the djinn's faces, they were equally as stymied.

Grimm muttered, "That witch thought he was going to break through this?"

Duke shrugged. Then they both leaned forward as the chest cracked open, creaking on its hinges.

My jaw dropped. There really was a treasure. Gold and silver coins of varying sizes, gem-studded brooches and other jewelry, crosses and rings, and as Cade sifted through, several loose gems cut to shine brilliantly, even in the faint light of the crescent moon. It hadn't been real, only an idea, until now.

The djinn crowded closer.

Cade's jaw tightened, but he allowed it even as he turned to me. "Callista wanted all the gems?"

"Yes," I said after I shut my mouth. I'd never seen such nakedly extravagant wealth in my life. Morris had had several of these hoards? And Cade had taken them…and wanted to make *me* heir?

"That will be the one she wants," Duke said, interrupting my spinning thoughts. He sounded tired and looked regretful as he pointed to one of the smaller ones, small enough to be hidden in my closed fist. It was hard to tell in the darkness, but it might have been different shades of blue or purple.

"Then that's the one she can't have." Grimm snatched it.

"Hey!" I reached for her hand, only to have mine go numb when she went misty and my hand passed through.

Both djinn stared at my protest.

"Give it to me. I can't fuck this up," I said.

"You already have, or you wouldn't have called on us." Grimm smiled. "Nasty bit of business that witch was, but fun. Does Callista have an inventory?"

"I don't know," I admitted. "But I don't want to risk it."

"Too bad. We're keeping this one and…this." She plucked an even smaller one from the bunch, a grey sphere with flashes of color I couldn't make out in the dark. "That leaves you with ten gems and a whole chest full of baubles to take back to her. It's not your fault if one of them isn't the one she wants. Except that it is. Oh well."

With a mocking flutter of her eyelashes, the djinni disappeared with both gems in her clutches.

Blood drained from my face as Duke shrugged.

"A deal is a deal." He shimmered as he shifted planes and was gone.

"Fuck," I muttered. How many times was I going to get screwed out of what I needed to get myself—and Cade—free? "Now what?"

Cade grimaced. "Now we take what remains back to Callista and pray we can buy her off with wealth rather than value."

Panic rose in me. "What if we can't? I did not bust my ass and almost lose you to—"

"I know, love. I know. But we have the treasure, Alejandro is behind us for now, and Callista just said to bring her the gems." He gestured at the glittering haul in front of us. "There are ten there with no way for us to know whether any are what she sought or if the djinn were correct in their estimation. I don't know how close she and Morris were, but he was an even cagier bastard than most. I doubt he would have told her what was actually in the chest, beyond taunting her with the existence of a soul gem."

"Which *isn't there* if that's what the djinn took!"

He just eyed me, a long, patient look that asked what either of us could do about it, and I slumped, suddenly far too tired.

"I can't," I muttered. "I can't do any more tonight."

"We have to stay ahead of Alejandro, assuming he's alive, and Callista is always short on patience. Give me the keys."

"You can drive?"

Cade shrugged. "Perhaps not as well as you, but yes, I've driven a vehicle on occasion. And could glamour any law enforcement who sought a license."

I looked at the starlit sky, trying to decide if I had the energy to fight him on this. I didn't. I had nothing left. I didn't even have the right treasure to buy my freedom. What I had was him and the offer he'd laid between us. I decided to trust him and have faith in our ability to find a way out of this. I handed over the keys.

"Thank you," he said. "I'll drive until sunrise so you can sleep."

"Okay."

I trudged back to the car and got in while he loaded the chest in the back—and crashed out asleep before he even got the engine turned on.

Chapter 15: Lya

The next time I woke, light was just greying the horizon.

"Ly?" Cade said.

I stretched, groaning at the pinch in my neck and muscles tightened by sitting too awkwardly for too long in a cramped space. "I'm awake."

"Good." He scrubbed a hand over his face. "I need to switch with you soon."

"Pull off at the next petrol station. We probably need to fill up. Where are we?"

From his annoyed expression, he hadn't considered fuel. "Almost to Creedmoor? I followed signs west but not to Raleigh."

"Good," I said, while cursing the fact that I'd only had about three or four hours of sleep. I needed a lot more after everything we'd been through, but that'd have to do. Given the back roads and small towns we'd have been passing through, I was doubly glad he'd been at the wheel. A white man driving at that time of night was less likely to get hassled than someone with my darker tones if we'd passed through one of the sundown towns Shonda had warned me about when I first arrived.

Shonda. I wondered how my friend was doing. I hadn't answered any of her messages in the last few months, not wanting to make her a target if anyone had managed to hack my phone. I couldn't afford to reach out now either, even if we did need a place to stay.

"Pull in there." I pointed to the Citgo sign to the left, leaning over to check the gauge. The little yellow light was on, and I bit my tongue to stop from scolding him at how close we'd come to being stranded with a ridiculous amount of liquid wealth in the truck. He must have been entirely focused on getting us away from Alejandro, given his main concern was usually for my safety.

The place was just opening, so I took a minute to text Callista. *I've got the treasure. Will be in later today.*

I didn't hear back, so that left me time to think. "We need a plan."

Cade's grip tightened on the wheel, loosening before I had to remind him he could probably dent it. "Is this the part where you tell me you're taking it in alone?"

"I'm tempted. But no." I leaned over the center console to rest my head on his shoulder. "I'm thinking the weres."

"Terrence and Ximena?"

"Terrence, at least. His name was on the note Callista gave me."

"Is that wise? Won't that mean he's working for her?"

I sighed and let my eyes settle closed for a few moments to think. "I don't know. But we have to stay in Durham. We can't take you to Raleigh, and neither of us can go near Chapel Hill in case Brennan's managed to report back to the Captain or the queens, or worse, fly back ahead of us."

"You should have killed him. Was one more count of treason really going to make a difference when there are already two hanging over you?"

"I don't know. He doesn't know the full story. I could get off on lesser misinformation and accessory charges." I sighed, knowing it was pointless because Cade was right, regardless of the technicalities, but I had to hold on to something. "It depends on who knows what. If Callista told the queens about the sirens like she did me, then it's their error. I don't know. I can't see how to fix everything."

He rested his head on mine. "We'll get through it. Starting with the wereleopard."

"Yeah?"

"I can't think of a better idea. We both need to rest. Callista will be expecting you to go straight to her, so I'll need a refuge for the day, and you'll need a fallback location."

"Exactly. Okay. You think they'll let you stay?"

"Only way to find out is to ask."

Sighing, I scrubbed my eyes again and sat up to make the call.

"You've reached Little." His voice was a deep, slow Southern drawl. In the background were the sounds of a car garage maybe, whirring from tools and the rumble of engines. Early for that, but maybe they opened early or stayed open late for Othersiders.

"Terrence?"

"Yes ma'am, that's me. Who's calling?"

"Hi, my name is Lya. I'm coming in from the other side of the state."

"Hang on a moment." The crackling sound of someone covering a mic came through, and when he was back, it was quieter. "I assume Miss Callista gave you my number."

"She did."

"Faction?"

"Half-elf. Exiled, not local. On task for her."

"Mm-hmm. Why do I have a feeling you're about to make a troublesome sort of request?"

I winced. "Because I am. I'm sorry, but I need a place to stay for a day or two."

"Just you?"

"Me and a vagabond."

"Y'all can't lodge in Raleigh?"

"No. It's complicated."

"So you're finna bring complication to me and mine."

There wasn't much I could say to that other than, "Yes. Like I said, I'm sorry. I can pay though."

Cade said, "Both of us can. I'll pay double the usual forfeit, in meat or cash, for a day's sleep in a dark room."

The were on the other end considered that. "Give me ten minutes to talk it over with my partner. This number good to call y'all back on?"

"Yes," I said. "I need to fill up, so if I don't answer, I'll call right back."

"That's fine. Talk soon."

I hung up and dropped my phone in the cupholder after plugging it in to charge. "I suppose that could have gone worse."

"Much," Cade agreed. "You're going to pay out of the cache?"

"If you don't mind, and if they'll take it. Callista said she knew I'd have to pay someone off, and so far all we've lost are a few gems."

He leaned in for a kiss. "What's mine is yours, love."

The lights came on inside the station, and Cade pulled us around to the pump nearest the exit. I got out and kept my head down as I filled the tank, not wanting to risk a vampire and petrol. Accidents would be flammable, and fire was one of the few things that could make him real dead. He could sext and he could drive, but no need to push our luck.

That done, I ducked inside to use the bathroom and grab a few protein bars from the Corner Grocery attached to the station. I hated the highly processed shit, but they were out of jerky. The elf-blooded needed a high protein balance, and I needed much more, given how frequently I was donating to Cade lately.

My phone rang as I got back in the car. I grimaced when it wasn't Terrence but Callista.

"Ma'am," I said when I answered.

"So you've got my treasure?"

"I do. I'm on my way back with it."

"I hear there were some complications. The kind that involve missing elves and angry queens. We had an agreement, girl."

The phone blipped with a call waiting. I ignored it as my stomach twisted. "I know."

"So. You bring Cade back against my command. Elves go missing after I tell the Darkwatch you'll be my eyes and their whipping girl, and as if that's not enough, the one remaining elf calls in the remnants of a siren on a beach. Oh, and also lays assault charges against you for downing him." She snorted. "You're stronger than I thought, or that upjumped Sequoyah is more foolish. Either way, it's trouble for me."

An unspoken, *What are you going to do about it?* hung between us as I tried to find the courage to say something.

"What will make this right?" I finally managed.

"I haven't decided yet," she snapped. "For now, you'd best pray I find what I need in that treasure, or all of this is coming out of your hide. Literally. And girl? I wouldn't advise seeking sanctuary in Raleigh. I just happened to speak to Torsten last night. You might have killed Morris, but Torsten doesn't look kindly on Cade's earlier attempt."

The call ended. I sat there, trying to remember how to breathe as I trembled with unspent adrenaline. In the passenger seat, Cade started to speak then shut his mouth when I shook my head.

"Don't," I whispered.

We'd both had the best of intentions in going to the Outer Banks and making the decisions we had there. The problem was, the fallout from those decisions was always going to land on me, whether it was my fault or not. Whether it was *fair* or not.

What would that mean for me if I was formally Cade's solidaire? How much love and treason and treasure was my life worth? Telling myself I'd probably be dead by siren attack if he hadn't come up with Alejandro was difficult just now, when I was probably going to end up in Callista's basement dungeon anyway.

I couldn't think about that yet. I needed to call Terrence back and sort out a safe haven for the day then get over to Callista's and face the utter fuck-up I'd made of my shot at freedom.

"There she is," Terrence drawled when I called him back. "Ximena's amenable to your request, for triple the usual forfeit. Each. Seems Miss Callista has had a bug up her ass lately, and we have a funny feeling it's something to do with you. She wouldn'a given you my number if I wasn't meant to help you, but we ain't finna be cub-foolish about this."

Cade grimaced when I glanced at him but nodded.

"Understood and accepted. One day and night of secure lodgings, starting when we arrive, in exchange for triple the usual forfeit times two."

He gave me an address north of the city proper and I repeated it back. "That's it. See you when we see you."

"Thank you. Should be fairly soon, we're only in Creedmoor."

"Good doing business with you." His tone shifted to one more teasing. "Stay out of trouble now, ya hear?"

The call ended before I could respond. I took another minute to gather myself before putting the car in gear and getting us back on the road. Twenty more minutes, assuming nothing happened.

Of course something happened.

We'd barely been driving ten minutes when a trio of black SUVs—just like the one whose tires I'd slashed on Ocracoke—barreled out from a small state road to box me in as we approached the interchange where US-15 became I-85. One sped up to get in front of me, and two more tucked in behind. Another petrol station flashed by before we were back to a narrow road through heavy trees.

"Shitting hell." I knew who they were even before glancing in the rearview mirror. It was hard to see more than that the driver behind was a blond woman and the passenger was a dark-haired man, but only one group had the precision, the information, and the motivation to pull this off.

Cade twisted in his seat, trying to see them. "Who—"

"It's the Darkwatch. Has to be. This is their last chance to bag me or the treasure or both before we reach the edge of werecat territory. Callista probably told them the same thing she did me, just bring her the gems. If they don't grab it now, they've lost two Darkwatch agents to a half-elf and a vampire on a fool's errand."

I evaluated my options, scanning the road. My stomach sank as I found it empty, which I had to assume was unusual for this time on a Monday morning given this was a main road into the Triangle. That was the other reason this had to be the Darkwatch—they had the clout inside human agencies to get a portion of a roadway temporarily shut down or divert drivers in anticipation of an accident they knew was coming because they were about to cause it.

I could try brake-checking the car behind us, but their trucks were bigger than mine and if they didn't give a shit about rear-ending me, I'd achieve nothing. The shoulder was nonexistent, the road edging into a narrow strip of grass before becoming brush and trees. Then even that was gone, and a guardrail popped up.

"Fuck, fuck, fuck." My eyes darted, searching for an option. A narrow state road to the left presented itself, and I wrenched the steering wheel to swerve onto it. Cade gripped the door hard enough that something creaked, and with a squeal of tires, the two SUVs behind us tried to follow. They were bigger and heavier than mine, so one spun on a road slick with dew from the lake I was now flying past, but the other fishtailed and made the turn.

Definitely after us.

The old asphalt was badly patched, and I swerved around a pothole before flooring the pedal. The SUV behind us hit it and bounced before they accelerated as well.

"Figure out where this road goes!" I snapped.

Gritting his teeth, Cade checked his phone. "Fuck."

"What?"

"It doesn't."

"What are you—"

"The road doesn't go anywhere. It ends."

"There's no way back onto the highway? No crossing road?"

"There's Falls Lake, Lya! That's it."

I'd screwed us. There was only one way back to the freeway, and it was back the way we'd come, where at least one car of Darkwatch elves would be waiting. My options were to drive us into Falls Lake, turn around and pray we could outrun them, or fight. And the first two weren't options at all.

Fight it was. I'd already committed treason in the elves' view, and like Cade said, what was a little more? Grimacing, I slowed the car and hauled on the wheel to bring us around as fast as I dared.

"What are you doing?" Cade snarled.

"You want to go for a swim? I've had enough damn water for one week."

The driver of the other SUV, now in front of us, slammed on the brakes and swerved across the road, blocking my path. The passenger-side doors both opened, and two gun-toting elves spilled out. Their eyes widened as I hit the gas and accelerated, their guns coming up.

I swerved, aiming to go around behind the SUV. A shot shattered my passenger-side mirror, and Cade grunted.

"Cade?"

"I'm fine."

We'd just made the grass when the other SUV reversed into us.

The last thing that crossed my mind as my truck went off the road was that I might just get that rest I'd been needing.

Chapter 16: Cade

The other vehicle struck them at the corner of the front bumper, and the impact sent them lurching sideways. Lya's yelp cut off as her head slammed into the window with a sickeningly dull thud. Cade grabbed the wheel, only for the other truck to keep going until it had them pinned between it and a tree with the crunch of metal and the splintering of wood. Everything came to a bone-jarring halt that rattled Cade's brain in his skull and probably would have knocked the wind from him, had he been breathing.

The two elves who'd gotten out of their vehicle leveled their guns at him, and he snarled to show fangs, loosing his glamour. They hesitated before scrambling backward, avoiding his eyes, until one of the other two SUVs came down the road and pulled to a halt where they could trap Lya's and point weapons from behind the open doors.

"Get out!" the man pointing a gun at him shouted. "Now and slowly. You move wrong, we shoot."

Cade didn't do a damn thing. They might be loaded for vampire. They might not. He was willing to take the risk to stay between them and Lya. All he needed to do was wait for one of them to slip and look him in the eye.

A tall, blond elf with pale skin and icy blue eyes approached, unhurried and almost buoyant, from the second car. He knocked on the hood of Lya's car and pointed his gun at Cade. Then, with a cocky smile, he shifted his aim to Lya's head. "Shut off the engine and get out, or I kill her here and now. Callista remanded her to us, and she won't give a shit what we do with her."

The first elf snapped around to look at the newcomer, opened his mouth, and then seemed to swallow his tongue as the blond aiming at Lya muttered a word Cade couldn't catch, probably elvish. A Sequoyah then, one more capable—and likely more ruthless—than Brennan at the beach had been.

"Engine off and get out, vampire. I won't tell you again," the Sequoyah said. "We were promised the bitch, and we're taking the gold as weregild, given two of ours are missing and there's blood on the beach."

Fury crested in Cade as he obeyed, moving as slowly as he could and squinting in the light of the sun as his door creaked. He'd have a burn later, but it didn't matter. The only thing that did was Lya. She'd been mad at him. Or frustrated, at least. Something not good, something he wouldn't want to be her last thought or feeling about him. She couldn't die now, not before he'd had a chance to fix things.

Not before he'd had a chance to do better by her.

"Hurt her, and you all die," he snarled.

"That would put you in an even trickier position than you already find yourself." The blond elf muttered something, more elvish.

The dark-haired one gasped. "Leith, you son of a—"

"Shut the hell up." Leith turned, jerking his head at one of the elves from his vehicle and the third from the first one. "Get the chest and load it in my truck." Mocking blue eyes flicked over Cade as he said, "Get the bitch as well and secure her for trial."

When Cade tensed, Leith shook his head. "Ah-ah, careful. You seem attached to her. Be a shame if you had to watch her die. Or would you try turning her? Can you turn someone missing part of their head?" The elf grinned, and his grip tightened on his gun. "You know, it's almost worth killing her just to see what you'd do, vampire. Less of a pain in the ass for us to transport her too. All roads end in death for her anyway."

Two elves hurried past with the treasure chest, and Cade clenched his fists so hard his nails bit into his palms. He needed that to buy Lya's freedom, but at the moment, he didn't even have his own. There were too many elves, two triads of high-blood Darkwatch agents with a third somewhere back up the road. They were elite, and this one, at least, was ruthless.

Maybe a bargain. "How much?"

Leith's eyebrows shifted in a frown. "For what?"

"Her."

The elf laughed nastily. "Nothing. She's worthless, except to get you to back off."

Cade let his helpless rage slither forth into a renewed glamour.

"Knock it off, or I kill the girl and spell you into paralysis to die in the sun." Leith tilted his head and smiled. "You can try for one of us, but we're loaded with silver. Someone will down you before you can save her, and then we'll kill her in front of you simply because you've irritated me."

There was no pleasure in this elf's avoidance of his gaze, and Cade watched as they leaned into the passenger-side door, unbuckled Lya, and dragged her limp body out.

First Alejandro had threatened her, then the sirens, now these elves.

Something broke in Cade, clutching at his heart with cold fingers at the idea that he couldn't keep her safe. Something that felt like the despair he'd sunk into during the early years in Morris's hands when he'd realized he was helpless against his sire's abuses and threatened to warp into the darkness that'd overtaken him when he'd freed himself.

"Put her with me as well," Leith ordered.

The other elves obeyed, eyes flicking warily to Cade as one took Lya's shoulders and another took her feet.

"She's cute. For a low-blood whoring herself to a vampire anyway." Leith winked as he walked backward, the gun trained on Cade now. "Might not be when we're done with her, but that depends on you. Stay the fuck away and be happy my orders are to stay out of Callista's arrangement with the Master of Raleigh."

Anguish threatened to buckle Cade's knees as he watched the elves pile into their cars and pull away. He didn't give a damn for the treasure beyond what it meant for Lya, and the blood curse he hadn't lifted when he'd unlocked the chest would take care of them if they opened it and took something, twisting their purpose against them. It was why he'd reluctantly accepted the djinn taking the soul gems.

But Lya...

He had to get her back. It was his fault this had all gone so terribly wrong. Maybe if he'd told her everything up front rather than trying to be so damned clever, none of this would have happened. She wouldn't be injured in the hands of enemies who would happily do her more harm. They might be celebrating right now, rather than him here alone, regretting their last interaction overflowing with frustration and anger.

Cade needed to see if he could get Lya's car going and into Durham. Safety waited for him there, and any vampire in his right mind would write off the loss of treasure and Lya both and simply move on. It wasn't his first battle lost over the long years, and it wouldn't be his last. Lya hadn't given him an answer on being his solidaire either, which was the only reason a vampire would risk themself in a situation like this.

But solidaire or not, he loved her.

And that meant he was getting her back, even if it meant war in the Triangle. Nobody would take her from him. Nobody.

First he needed to get out of here.

He eyed Lya's car, decidedly crunched in front where it'd been pinched by the elven SUV on one side and the tree on the other. At least they'd left him a way out. He wasn't sure if it was safe to drive the damn thing though or what the sign of it being unsafe would be, other than it catching on fire. Having watched Morris burn, he had absolutely no desire to discover its unsafety that way.

The weres.

It'd have to be them. The Raleigh coterie was out. Even if he could convince Maria to help him, Lya had formally ended their blood contract, and Callista had tattled to Torsten about him. Callista herself didn't give a damn, considering all she had to do now was demand the gems she wanted from the elven queens.

As he reached back in the car for Lya's phone and unplugged it, he tried not to worry himself with why the Darkwatch would want a half-elf most of the elves in the area despised. He hadn't liked the sense he'd gotten of any of the Sequoyah elves in the last few days but told himself that wasn't his to worry about either. All he needed to think about right now was getting back on the road and getting Lya back.

He moved to where the car would shade him from the sun, swiped a thumb over her phone, glad he knew the pattern lock, and tapped to her last call.

"Here so soon?" the same smooth, masculine voice as before answered.

"Terrence."

"Vagabond?"

"That's me. We've run into one of those complications."

"Mm-hmm. Lemme guess, y'all wanna buy some additional assistance."

"I do. Do you know of a discreet mechanic?"

Terrence snorted. "So happens that several of my people are. What happened?"

Grimacing, Cade debated how much to say. "Some of Lya's kin took exception to something she did. They ambushed us on US-15. She pulled off onto a side road, and they disabled her vehicle."

"Sounds like we best send a tow then. Can you keep mundanes away?"

"Yes. How much?"

"This is actually in our wheelhouse, and I'm assuming your girl's people got what they wanted or you wouldn't be calling, so standard rates. Might give you a discount if you bring the repair to my garage. But don't expect us to fight your battle for you and don't bring it to my doorstep."

"Done," Cade said quickly. Better to deal with the werecat pride than anyone else in the local Otherside community. The Triangle's bizarre three-way power sharing agreement did have its perks.

"Text me a screenshot of your location. I'll have somebody out ASAP."

The call ended, and Cade did as instructed before slumping down to sit in the dirt, miserable with sunburn and Lya's loss and trying desperately to come up with a plan.

***

The werecat body shop was more or less what Cade had expected as they pulled into the dirt yard: a boxy concrete building with a garage attached, looking like it was just hanging on, with rusting older vehicles lined up off to one side. They might well have a prosperous business front here, but it made sense for them to downplay it. It drew less attention from the mundanes, and it let the stronger elf and vampire factions feel secure in overlooking the joined leopard-jaguar pride. There was safety in being overlooked.

"Thanks for the lift," he said to Malik.

The dark-skinned wereleopard grunted, and the sun shone on his bald head as he turned to Cade. "Boss wants you to meet him inside to arrange payment before I do anything else."

"Understood." He swung down from the high cab of the tow truck, pulling his cap down, glad to have found sunscreen in Lya's abandoned purse. He'd still have a burn from today—it was already itching, badly—but at least it wouldn't get worse.

A small woman with black hair, sienna-brown skin, and broad features started to greet him as he walked in. She tilted her head and sniffed, her mouth dropping slightly after a moment in a Flehmen response.

"Ah. Our stray," she said with a Southern accent before switching to Spanish and hollering toward the back. She smiled as she turned back to him. "Not every day we get your kind round here."

"I can imagine," Cade said. "Ximena, I presume?"

She nodded, her eyes not meeting his but not leaving him either.

Cade introduced himself as quiet footsteps announced the arrival of Terrence. The wereleopard was only a little taller than his counterpart, whip-lean with a wiry strength, with dark umber skin and eyes the color of tiger-eye gems. Cade raised his eyebrows at the Marine tattoo on the man's arm. That wasn't just impressive for having been a Marine; it was more so for his having been a were in the human armed forces, speaking to excellent control over his cat in difficult and bloody situations. No wonder he was in charge at his relatively young age.

"Terrence," Cade said. "I'm much obliged to you both for your assistance in this unusual situation."

Terrence studied him, scenting much as Ximena had before answering. "We know what it is to be pushed out and in need of help. We won't be doormats in offering it, and we won't offer it cheaply when you can afford it. But we will offer it."

Cade smiled. "A plain talker. I appreciate that."

"Saves on trouble. Now, why don't you come on to the back, and we'll get your payment sorted out."

He followed Terrence, feeling Ximena's eyes on him the whole way. Rumor had it the two were lovers as well as business partners, defying tradition—and for some wereclans, law— saying like had to seek like to ensure the births of more weres. Turning by bite was forbidden under the Détente, since it'd allow the weres to grow far faster than the elves, who could only reproduce sexually, or the vampires, who couldn't grow faster than the population they fed on.

Maybe these two understood him better than he'd recognized before.

Terrence's small office held only a battered desk and three old chairs. The laptop on the desk looked newer than everything else though, as did the card reader. "So," he said, drawing the word out. "Your friend—"

"Girlfriend." If Terrence was speaking plainly and honestly, so would Cade.

"Oh, lordy. Okay. You heard the terms she negotiated?"

"I did. I can pay for both of us now, plus the cost of the tow, the repairs, and…call it a tip in appreciation of your willingness to help two outsiders."

"Huh. Vagabonds are that rich?"

Cade shrugged, worried about having shown his hand but more concerned with wrapping this up so that he could go after Lya. "We are when we started life as pirates and can glamour wealth managers into looking the other way."

Shaking his head, Terrence looked around at his small office before scribbling a number on a piece of paper and sliding it over. "The varying lives we lead. Fine. Cash, credit, something else?"

The figure would be enough to buy a three-bedroom house in a nice part of the Triangle, but it was worth it. Anything to get Lya back. And besides that, Cade had lived through the period of US chattel slavery and all the subsequent periods in which people who looked like him did everything in their power to strip anything and everything from people who looked like Terrence. The immigrant werewolf clans had done more or less the same toward both native and less powerful wereanimal groups. Terrence's people—the wereleopards and the Black human he appeared to be—were owed and then some. Cade wasn't going to quibble over this, especially not when the smallest local factions were the ones generous enough to help.

Shifting to one hip, Cade pulled out his wallet and held up a black metal card. The wereleopard took it, brows lifting at its weight, then pulled an old-fashioned card imprinter out of his desk.

"I'ma charge you now for the tow and repairs," he said as he flipped a piece of paper on top, ran the roller over it all, and imprinted the card number. "The rest comes in irregular installments so the IRS isn't on my damn ass for money laundering or some shit."

"Call me if there's fallout from this." Cade loosed his glamour just long enough to let his eyes flash to black before tamping it down again as Terrence's eyes flickered to the peridot of his leopard. "I wouldn't want your assistance here to cause trouble."

"Pleasure doing business, then." Terrence slid the card back over then offered his hand to shake when Cade had tucked the card away. "You'll stay with me. I won't put the danger of this on any of my people. My second, Lola, will drop you off and leave you with a courtesy car. Trash that car like you did the mess out front, and I'll add it to your bill. We good?"

"Good. Thank you again."

"Don't mention it. Seriously." Rising, he gestured Cade out of the office, singing as he followed.

Ximena looked up from her conversation with a small, slight, light-brown-skinned girl with short-cropped curls and eyes as dark as Cade's own.

"He's singing 'Mo Money Mo Problems,' so you must've been good for it," Ximena said. A pinch Cade hadn't noticed at first eased from between her brows as she glanced at Terrence, who nodded and turned to the girl.

"Lola, meet Cade," Terrence said. "He'll be my guest for the next twenty-four hours. Give him the black Challenger and drive him to my place. Have Malik follow you over. Then come on back here when you're done. You got homework to finish, girl."

"Yes, Terrence." Lola looked far too young to be a werecat's second, but she seemed like an old soul. Maybe she was more than she appeared.

Cade inclined his head respectfully, noting Ximena's approving nod out of the corner of his eye.

As he followed Lola out, he turned his mind to the next step in his plan to get Lya back.

Chapter 17: Cade

Cade sat at the edge of the bed in the spare half of Terrence's duplex. The place had blackout curtains, which were now mercifully shut against the daylight that tugged at Cade's mind and body almost as much as his need to go after Lya did. Lola had shown him around, pointing to the bathroom, the kitchen, and so on in a firm voice and pressing a spare key into his hand. The stern look she'd given him when she'd warned him not to lose it or bring trouble back would have been laughable on most people her age, but he took her seriously and promised to keep it with him.

He inhaled and blew the breath out, shaking his head and trying to focus on the plan he'd come up with. He needed rest, but the powerful blood he'd taken over the last few days would keep him going a little longer.

First, he had to see Callista.

It would be a risk, but nothing in the territory moved without her say-so, and if it did, there was hell to pay, as he was learning the hard way. She didn't want Cade here and going after the treasure himself, but here he was anyway. Addressing that might get him some wiggle room.

After that, he had two hard roads to choose from. One, calling Torsten's second, Aron, with the lie that Lya was his solidaire and the truth that the elves had taken her, and trying to gain assistance there. Or two, going after her alone and risking the elves lashing out at Torsten's coterie. They wouldn't care that Cade was a vagabond. If he was in the territory, he was ultimately Torsten's responsibility, which put everyone in a tight spot.

The third road he'd already rejected.

He wouldn't just leave. He'd fucked everything up by not telling Lya he was coming in the first place, and now he had to fix it. Underneath all that was a simmering, resentful rage that it had even been an issue for him to come. Otherside didn't have much space for people to exist outside carefully defined boxes and accepted behaviors or rituals. And the more time he spent with Lya, watching her be set up for failure time and again in a system she had pointed out was working as intended, the more he wanted to simply burn it all down.

But he couldn't. It was just him and her, and for now, he didn't even have her.

Time to change that, even if there'd be blood on the floor or in someone's mouth before the night ended. With the mood he was in, he welcomed it. Opened up to the flicker of darkness he'd learned at Morris's hands and kept oh-so-carefully leashed with a need to survive and a craving for Lya's trust. He didn't know what he was going to do yet, but visiting Callista should open or close some options.

Although the delay chafed at his nerves, Cade took a quick shower and changed his clothes. Appearing before Callista dirty and bedraggled would give her the upper hand and speak too much to Cade's desperation. He needed to look in control—wronged but not with his back completely against the wall. Torsten was much the same, preferring a neat appearance and a polite tongue, so if he did go to Raleigh afterward, the cost in time would be made up in actually gaining an audience.

He hoped.

Slathered in sunscreen and freshly dressed in clean jeans and a white button-down shirt, Cade hurried out of his borrowed lodgings and locked up behind him. The drive to Callista's bar was quick, and he took another deep inhale as he parked and strode up to the door.

The head bitch herself glared at him from behind the bar as he stepped inside, her green eyes seeming to spark with fury.

Conversation in the bar dwindled as Cade approached her, and a couple people hurried out.

"Callista," he said in a low voice, allowing a hint of a growl into it. "Might I have a word?"

She smiled, the venom in it matching her glare perfectly. "No."

"I'm afraid I must insist."

Pinpricks danced over his skin, and a few more people made hasty exits.

"I have no business with you, Cade."

"Yes, you do." He offered his own dangerous smile, one considerably sharper than hers. "Your little puppets have abducted my solidaire and stolen something she went to great pains to acquire for you." The lie left his tongue so easily it felt like truth, and Cade hoped she read the clench of his jaw as determination rather than the *oh fuck* feeling curling through his gut. If Lya didn't agree, he'd just committed a killing offense for both of them. But if he did nothing, both of them were already dead anyway.

Callista's expression hardened even further, and the prickling sensation grew. "Back office. Now."

He inclined his head and followed her, standing with arms crossed when she didn't offer him a seat.

"What the fuck is this about little Lydia being your solidaire?" she demanded. "When was that registered?"

"It hasn't been. Yet."

"Then there's no grievance."

"There is if I say there's one." He loosened his grip on his glamour just enough to let his pupils expand too wide, as much a threat as showing fangs would be, if more civil.

Callista's eyes narrowed. "Even if it was registered, Torsten would rather flay you as an example of what happens to vampires who attempt to kill their masters than enforce your claim with the Conclave."

Cade tilted his head. "There's something I've been wondering about since you first called Lya. Why do this the hard way?"

"What are you talking about?"

"Oh, don't play coy. You're too old for it and so am I." He sneered, unable to help the expression even if it put her back up even further. "Is this a deeper play against the elves? You want them to take the blood curse for you?"

Something flickered in her eyes.

"Ah. You didn't know about the curse." He took the seat she hadn't offered, a power move that might get him killed but might also get him some respect. "Morris had a pet blood witch for a while. Only Morris and those of his bloodline can handle the treasure safely. With the old bastard and all of his other fledglings dead, two people remain. Me. And my solidaire."

At least, Cade prayed that Lya could handle it safely. He'd only given her the two swallows of blood to save her life, and it'd been months ago. She might have taken enough to be a carrier for the vampire virus, or the elven antibodies in her own blood might have fought it off. He couldn't be sure until it was too late, unless he managed to get her consent to the arrangement and feed her again first.

"You seriously expect me to believe you took a half-elf as a solidaire?" she said.

He shrugged. It was frowned upon, but he'd only be in trouble if he actually turned her. "Believe it or don't. I opened the chest, but I didn't lift the curse. Lya doesn't know about it."

He smiled nastily. "Now, I would have been happier not telling you any of that, but I'm hoping we can still come to a more sensible arrangement. One that returns my solidaire, gets you whatever the hell it is you're after, and lets us all part ways peacefully."

Stone-faced, Callista took her seat on the opposite side of the desk. "There are other blood witches."

"I'm well aware." Another reason to move quickly—if the djinn hadn't killed or seriously injured Alejandro, he'd be on his way back here, for revenge or the treasure or both. "I'm also aware of how expensive their services can be. Again, Callista, why are you making this so much more difficult than it needs to be? If you'd told me you wanted it to pay off Lya's debt, I would have fetched it to you myself." He couldn't help his smirk. "Mami Wata and I go back a long time."

Her lip twitched in the beginnings of a snarl before she smoothed her face. "That wasn't the deal I wanted."

"So Lya was right then. You never intended her to come home alive. The debt was to be paid in blood and gold both."

Callista shrugged, her lips curling in a mocking smile. "It's all currency. Some find blood more valuable than others. But no. Lya was to pay off her debt to me in treasure, and the one you incurred in following her as an indenture to the Darkwatch if she survived its retrieval." She tilted her head. "Surely you noticed the sirens preferred her? The Darkwatch was just there to clean up the mess and bring me whatever was left if she didn't survive the sirens or that arrogant bitch Mami Wata."

"And me? None of that says why I couldn't have come from the beginning."

"*You* would have stopped her from giving the sirens what they wanted, and you give her ideas above her station that make her harder to control. None of this would have become such a fuck-up if you'd stayed out of it." She smiled again, sweetly venomous. "You have only yourself to blame for all of this."

Suddenly, the fights, the daylight, the long travel, and the stress of losing Lya all weighed too heavily on Cade, and he lost his patience for this game. "I want her back," he snapped, "and I want her undamaged or as undamaged as she can be after being in a car accident and dragged off by the Darkwatch. Now, Callista. End of story."

She steepled her fingers, pure, joyful malice in her expression and tone. "We don't always get what we want. Take me, for example. I'm still waiting for my treasure. Which means I need to make a few calls. You can see yourself out, Cade. Try not to run into any of Torsten's people. Or maybe you want to try telling *them* she's your solidaire, hm?"

No. He wasn't going to just walk out.

He let a little more of the darkness within him rise to the surface, baring his fangs in an open threat. He was certain she knew who he'd been before the masters of New York and Miami had put an end to it. Apparently a reminder was in order.

Callista rose and leaned forward across the desk.

The room dimmed with shadow, and the musky scent of a woodland predator teased through the room—not were but something bigger and darker and much, much older. Something that sent primeval alarm bells ringing in Cade's brain and had him out of his chair hunched in a fighting stance before he realized what he was doing.

"Don't press me, *moroi*. I'm older than you know and more powerful than you can comprehend. Count yourself lucky my quarrel isn't with you and get the fuck out while I allow it."

Cade took a step back toward the door then another as despair rose to take the place of rage and made him desperate. "Where did they take her? Give me that, and I'll lift the curse for you when you get the treasure back. No need to spend money, favors, or time on finding a blood witch."

Darkness rose in the room. Not the safety of night. Something else. Something alive.

His back hit the door as it seemed to reach for him, seeking the parts of him he kept locked away. The parts that remembered what it felt like to be hurt beyond comprehending, body and mind.

Then Callista was just Callista again, a small woman seated in her cracked leather chair. "You getting killed trying to play the shining knight gets me nothing. No."

He took a breath, trying to still his racing heart. There had to be a way. "It does if I leave a vial of my blood and instructions in a secure location."

Her eyes narrowed. "That's all it takes?"

"The *moroi* might not have magic like the elves, djinn, or witches, but we have glamour. There's magic in blood, and magic in the spell. It has to be my blood though, and if you warn the Darkwatch I'm coming, you don't get the spell." When she just stared at him, he pushed harder, heart thudding. "It's custom-made."

"How convenient."

"We both know Morris had the money and the paranoia to commission one."

Again, she stared at him, and this time, he held his tongue. *Tell me where she is, you bitch. Give me a chance.*

"Fine." She reached for a piece of paper and scribbled something on it before sliding it across the desk. "She might be here."

"Might? I'm not doing this for might."

"Then don't." Callista shrugged. "I don't give a fuck. I'll have what I want sooner or later, one way or another. It pleases me to have it sooner and easier, but your cooperation is a bonus, not a need, given you weren't supposed to be here at all."

Cade approached the desk slowly, wary of a trap and barely able to stop himself from snarling.

She sneered at his caution. "Leave the blood and the spell with Janae or Hope."

Glancing down at the paper, he found an address at the top and below it, "J/H" followed by a number with a local area code. "Thank you."

Callista smiled as though she didn't hear the way the bitter words nearly stuck in his throat—or maybe because she did hear them. "Don't wear out Terrence's hospitality, hm?" Her expression hardened. "And don't you dare think to cross mine again, or there will be no bargains. Now get out."

Paper in hand, Cade forced himself to walk at a normal pace out of the room then out of the now-empty bar. It wasn't until he was in the car and driving back to Terrence's that he remembered something: those making threats were very likely feeling threatened themselves.

What was Callista so afraid of that she'd reveal something of her true self—something he'd never heard so much of a whisper of before—and how did this treasure help her? How did soul gems help her? The damned things were forbidden under the Détente.

Ah. The creation of *new* soul gems was forbidden, as was their sale, transfer, and distribution. *Possessing* one was not. It was a fine line and one that she could tread by having everyone else do the dirty work of finding, acquiring, and moving a gem already in existence. The corrupt bitch had to be desperate to risk so many other people finding out what she was after, although it did add another reason why she wasn't particularly keen on Lya surviving the job or the elves retaining the treasure.

It also begged an interesting question: was there someone stronger than her?

He sighed as he pulled up in front of Terrence's duplex and went inside to prep what was needed to break the curse on the treasure.

The question didn't matter.

Lya did, even if she'd been mad at him. *Especially* if she'd been mad at him.

Focus. He had a feeling a Watcher would be on his tail until Janae or Hope, whoever they were, called to confirm receipt. Maybe until the treasure was back with Callista.

That was fine. Nothing mattered more than getting Lya back.

Chapter 18: Lya

I woke with a pounding head, cresting nausea, and enough pain that something felt broken. I was alone in a bare—hell, unfinished—room with exposed support beams and wiring sprouting from the walls, lying on a dusty concrete floor with my wrists tied behind me. I thought about sitting up but decided against it when shifting sent a searing pain through my head. The only light in the room coming from fluorescent bulbs overhead added to it, between their harsh glow and the annoying hum all fluorescents made.

Concussion. Couple of sprains. Definitely some bruising.

Cataloging my injuries could only distract me for so long. I didn't remember the journey here, but I did remember a few things: the impact and Cade, now trapped on a dead-end road in daylight with a car that was probably disabled.

If he'd survived the impact to his side of the car.

If the elves hadn't killed him to grab me or the treasure I was certain they'd stolen or just to be wankers.

If he wasn't injured and left for dead on that road, slowly crisping as the sun did too much damage for the vamp virus to repair.

My scrambled brain tortured me with image after image of all the ways he could be hurt, dying, or dead. And I'd been mad at him. He'd known it. He'd have scented it, my frustration and anger, the fact that I hadn't known if I wanted to be his solidaire.

Oh no. Cade.

I laid there in abject misery for a few more minutes. I needed to figure out where I was and how to escape, but as my mind marched through its horror parade, it was hard to care. Why had I hesitated to say yes to being his solidaire? Why had I been so harsh with him, when he'd only been trying to make sure I stayed alive? He'd offered me everything I craved from a relationship, and I hadn't had the courage to claim it.

The door opening jarred me out of my thoughts, and I jumped, wincing in pain and cursing at both that and the completely silent movement of a Darkwatch-trained high-blood. I didn't recognize this one, but the scent of our kind—rosemary and sage blended with the burnt marshmallow scent of a heavy Aether user—clung to him.

He crouched, studying me with icy blue eyes and a similarly cold demeanor. "Lydia of House Desmarais." My House name earned me a sneer. "Or at least, that's what we were told. Frankly, I don't see the point of giving halflings House names or bothering with exile, but I suppose that decision is above me for now."

None of that was a question, so I just glared at him and tried to get my brain back in order. Worrying about Cade would not protect me from this asshole, and if he was using slurs in addition to kidnapping me, I was in for a bad time. Farand had demonstrated that over the summer. I needed my wits. Shame the concussion had them bouncing around like a box full of ping-pong balls shot from a cannon.

The elf snorted. "Silent treatment. Don't worry. We can deal with that." He rose and, with a rough grip on my bicep, pulled me to sit upright. "Or is it the concussion?"

I choked down a heave as the room spun and did my best to glare, although my dizziness rendered it pretty ineffective. His pale skin, blond hair, and light eyes marked him as a scion of

House Sequoyah. He could easily heal all of my physical injuries with the lightest bit of Aether, but I had a feeling he was like Brennan—he liked physical pain in his victims. The evidence of it, the suffering of it. The twisting of a healing gift sickened me, even if I didn't expect it to be extended to myself.

"Why am I here?" I grated out, unable to hold it in any longer. I had an idea—trial—but if that was the case, I'd rather face it than fuck around like this.

"Oh, she *does* have a tongue. Fantastic." His demeanor became oily and self-satisfied. "We're collecting on the indenture Callista promised us, although I doubt there'll be much left to collect on after your trial." He grinned as the blood fled from my head, and I wavered. "You remember Brennan, right?"

The elf in question slipped into the room. Fury and pleasure blended into an expression that sent chills over me as he stared at me. "Hello, girly."

Now, that was just silly, enough to shift me out of wondering how long I'd been here for him to make it here from the coast when he'd been behind me and Cade with a disabled vehicle and a fucked-up leg. "'Girly?' Who the fuck—"

The Sequoyah's slap wasn't as hard as it could have been, but with the pain I was already in, I saw stars and toppled over heaving. My stomach was empty, but it did its best.

"She has a concussion," the one who'd hit me said pleasantly. "Should be fun."

Brennan made an agreeable noise. "Leith, Callista's on the phone. She wants a word about the treasure."

"Of course she does." Leith sighed and rose. "We'll finish up here later. No food, no water, no sleep. Leave the lights. Let's see what the Arbiter wants, and then we can see what we can get out of this one for the trial. Your testimony is good, but a confession is better if we want the queens to remand her to us for punishment." He eyed me with a dark look. "And we still need to find out what happened to Elias and Marc. All that blood on the beach and no bodies to recover."

"Sir."

They left together as soundlessly as they'd both arrived, and the lock clicked behind them, leaving me feeling even worse than I had when I'd first awakened. I knew that name—Leith. Not just any son of House Sequoyah. He was a prince. A lesser prince by blood, despite his power, but a dangerous one from the rumors I'd overheard at the bail bond office. Farand had hero-worshipped him, of course.

From those rumors, the very last thing I wanted was to be trapped here with him.

And he was definitely ruthless enough to leave no loose ends, especially if he'd found elven blood on the beach and Cade's bite marks in Brennan's throat. A full triple triad had come after us. If I was here, Cade had to be dead.

I was on my own.

New urgency stabbed through me, and the adrenaline helped clear the mental fog. I reached past my splitting headache for Aether just to see if I could—and found it. The arrogant assholes hadn't strapped me. I'd brought Brennan down at the beach, and they still didn't consider me enough of a threat to neuter my magic with the lead-lined silver cuffs all the Darkwatch carried. Yeah, I'd only half-managed the spell, partly because I wasn't as strong as a full-blooded elf but also because I'd been rushing and sloppy. But had Brennan really told them all I was weak enough not to need a cuff?

Things just got interesting.

First, I had to get out of this room. This had to be a temporary location or one where a frame job could be set up without compromising one of their preferred sites if things went badly. Either that or Leith was running this op partially under the radar, which made the whole situation even more dangerous.

I forced myself to one knee then to my feet, wobbling when a wave of dizziness hit and I couldn't use my arms for balance. Twisting, I almost rolled my eyes to find they'd secured me with what looked like plain, heavy-duty handcuffs. First, no neutering cuff. Second, no double-secure bindings. They should have used cuffs and zip-ties or rope or anything else in case I managed to free myself. Even I knew that.

Goddess, but it was good to be underestimated sometimes.

Unless this was a trap. I hesitated then decided, even if it was some kind of trap, I couldn't possibly be in more trouble than I already was. I leaned against a wood framing beam, searching for something I could use to pick the cuffs. I could try one of the wires as a last resort. But they looked too thick to fit in the keyhole, and if the overhead lights were on, they might be live. In a room as messy as this, there had to be something else.

There. Along the base of one wall, where it'd been overlooked by whoever had swept the space out, was a thin bit of what must've been soldering wire. The lead would hurt like hell to handle. I grimaced.

But my options were slim, and my time was running out by the second. Callista wasn't usually given to long conversations, and while the "no sleep" directive sounded like they had the time to try sleep deprivation to soften me, I didn't fancy waiting to find out if I'd have the night to get out of here before they got started on other methods.

I staggered over and sat with my back to the wall, fingers scrabbling for the piece of metal. One of my fingernails ripped as I dug it out of the crease between wall and floor, and between that and the immediate burn of lead, I swallowed down a curse. Twisting so I could see behind me, I did my best to shape the wire against the floor then maneuvered it into the lock.

My first two attempts failed.

The pick was fiddly, it was burning the fuck out of my fingers, I had to be extra careful not to let it press against the torn nail lest the lead get into my bloodstream and do Leith's torture for him, and adrenaline had me so amped that fine motor work was nearly beyond me.

I dropped the pick and forced myself to close my eyes.

To take a breath. Then another. Get my racing mind and galloping heart under control.

I could do this. I had to do this. Nobody was coming for me. With Cade dead, nobody gave one flying fuck about me.

Cade.

Another shaky breath. *No. Not now. Mourn later.*

I swallowed all the guilt and fear, wrapped my fingers in my shirt, and fumbled for the pick again. Another three tries and the cuff clicked open. Hurriedly, I opened the other before shoving my makeshift tool into the pocket of my shorts. They'd find it if they searched me, but I didn't intend to give them an opportunity to search me.

This was it. I'd escape or die trying.

Options. Kick the door down? Try to plow straight through a wall? I had no idea where I was or what this space was meant to be. No idea how thick the walls were or what was on the other side. I'd get one chance because once I started, the noise would bring my captors.

Be smart. For once in your life, be smart.

I crept to the door and pressed an ear to it. Voices echoed, sounding like they might be down a corridor or in a large space. There might be someone right outside standing guard, and I wouldn't know unless I tried breaking the door down.

They underestimated you so far. Would they bother placing a guard for a half-elf?

They might. Fuck. I didn't know how the Darkwatch operated on this side of the Atlantic. What I'd seen so far was sloppy, especially given the reputation of House Monteague, and I couldn't shake the feeling that something was wrong. Paranoia crawled down the back of my neck, feeling just like—

Like a tracking tag in close proximity to a target.

I stiffened then scrambled back. As I was trying to sort out what was instinct and what was magic, the lock clicked. The door swung open, and my jaw dropped.

No.

Alejandro slipped in and shut the door behind him, dropping a leather sack to the floor beside the door and already leering, despite a black eye and lacerations across his face and arms. But the grin shifted to true amusement and maybe a hint of respect as he took in the handcuffs on the floor.

"Idiots. Elves are always so overconfident." He eyed me with a dangerous twist to his expression. "You, lady, have caused me a good deal of trouble. The djinn were yours?"

I couldn't answer. My heart was pounding into my throat.

Leith on one side, Alejandro on the other, and I was trapped in this room.

"They must have been, since the treasure is here, along with you." He took a menacing step closer, his smile widening as I lurched away. "I owe you pain for that, and Leith is inclined to let me play with you before he gets started. Before that though, a question."

I just shook my head. "I don't know anything."

"You haven't even heard the question."

I shifted, trying to figure out how to get around him. He wasn't much bigger than me, but I was bleeding, and I'd literally be damned if the blood witch managed to catch a drop.

"Tell me, lovely lady, does the Darkwatch know about the curse on the treasure?"

That distracted me. "Curse?"

"Cade didn't tell you?" He chuckled richly. "Why do you think I still had the damnable thing in my possession for your djinn to track? I wasn't opening it, let alone touching a single piece of that gold, without breaking the curse first. The box hummed with it." Tilting his head, he studied me. "You really had no idea."

I shook my head, relieved he thought the djinn were tracking the chest itself rather than following an Aetheric tracking tag and siren's blood.

"Which means you can't have told the Darkwatch fools. Excellent." He rubbed his hands together. "Where is your knight errant, anyway?"

My throat closed up, and I gritted my teeth.

Alejandro arched an eyebrow. "Dead? True dead?"

"No." I snapped the word out, as much to anchor myself as defy the witch. "I don't know where he is."

"Not here, and that's all that matters. Another question."

"I've got nothing for you," I hissed.

"On the contrary. Did Cade ever give you his blood?"

The question seemed out of left field. I started to answer then pressed my lips firmly shut. I didn't owe him shit, and besides, I didn't know what the safe answer would be. Cade shouldn't have fed me because I'd been pretty damn drained when he had. Two swallows wasn't enough to turn me, fortunately, but I didn't know why else Alejandro would care unless it was to cause trouble.

He glided closer. "Come now. Don't make this more difficult." He shrugged. "Or do."

His hand darted out fast, and I tripped over my own feet dodging away. I managed to catch myself against the floor on my uninjured hand, fisting the one with the torn and bloody nail against my stomach.

"You think you can evade me?" His eyes shone with anticipation. "In a room this size? You can try, of course. Then we'll play."

If I could lead him away from the still-unlocked door, I might have a chance. The room was small, but he was amusing himself by toying with me. I darted, trying to fake him out, before I remembered something important.

I might be afraid of his magic, but I had my own.

Using it would alert the other elves, but not using it would put my body and blood in the hands of a man who wanted to abuse both.

I took a deep breath then opened myself to as much Aether as I could hold.

Chapter 19: Lya

As Alejandro lunged for me, I sent a lash of Aether toward his mind. "Stop!"

He halted where he was, a confused expression pinching his face.

When he opened his mouth, I pushed harder through the link I'd made to him and said, "Don't speak. Don't move. Stay here, no matter what happens."

Fury twisted his face then, and my heart hammered as I backed toward the door. Hauling it open, I threw myself into a corridor as unfinished as the room had been—and straight into the hands of the elfess guarding the door.

They weren't entirely stupid or sloppy then.

"I told him you could use Aether well enough to be a problem, low-blood or not," the elfess said. A Luna, from her dark hair and eyes and tan skin. Before I could do anything, she drew on twice as much Aether as I could hold and stung my aura so hard I howled and dropped to the floor.

"I also told him you'd find your way out of those cuffs," she muttered and frowned down at me. "Does he listen to me? No."

"What in the name of the Goddess is going on?" Leith's irate voice came from down the hall, where a larger space was illuminated by a fluorescent light and LED lanterns.

"The prisoner almost escaped," the elfess said, adding under her breath, "Like I said she would."

I dragged myself backward as Leith came around a corner and stalked toward us. "So she did. How resourceful." The scent of burnt marshmallow became overwhelming as he drew on Aether and pressure weighed on my bones with his strength. "Paralysis should fix that."

Magic hit my body in a searing lash.

My muscles stopped working. All of them. Not just my limbs, but my heart and diaphragm as well. I couldn't breathe. My heart sat heavy in my chest. And I had no way to scream from the terror of effectively being dead while living.

Leith joined the elfess, toeing me and smiling as though he liked watching my body flop. "You might live another two minutes if I don't lift this, so listen very closely. I just had an interesting conversation with Callista. She says the treasure is blood cursed, so that witch was telling the truth about his usefulness. Apparently, we should have taken the vampire as well, but Callista has a way around that."

He'd said pay attention, but the longer he monologued, the more black spots hovered at the edges of my vision and the faster I went quietly insane.

"I'll lift the paralysis. But you're going to co-operate, or I'll find a way to hurt you that won't compromise the witch's work."

A scrape at the door to the room I'd been in turned into Alejandro. My spell had worn off.

"You only need her alive," he rasped, glaring at me. "Assuming Cade gave her blood at some point."

Leith frowned. "Enervate."

My head seemed to explode as my heart thumped back to life then started racing, and I started hacking as my desperate inhale brought in dust. I curled into a knot, trying to convince myself I was still alive, only to get a kick in the back to send my diaphragm spasming again.

"Let's see how you like this," Leith said.

Cold metal closed around my left arm and pinched tight, digging into the flesh of my wrist. A magic-neutering cuff, one that hurt more than it should.

"Get her up and bring her. You come too, witch."

Brennan joined the elfess, each grabbing an arm as they dragged me in Leith and Alejandro's wake.

"You're gonna pay for that, bitch," Brennan muttered.

I was too busy focusing on living to reply.

The corridor opened into a huge, open space. Half-covered windows showed the setting sun over an isolated construction zone, although the stream of headlights in the distance said we were probably near I-40. We had to be in RTP, in some unfinished office space, not that knowing that helped me.

I was dropped in front of the gods-damned chest that'd started all this.

"Open it," Leith said.

I did, having watched Cade do so earlier and knowing where to put my fingers to trigger the hidden latch. Gold shone dully under the fluorescent lights, as did the handful of gems the djinn had rejected.

"Witch. What happens if she touches it and there's a curse?"

Alejandro's response lashed us with irritation. "Likely nothing, for now. Morris liked terror. Savored it like fine wine. Odds are he'd want something that came with creeping dread and long-term consequences."

"How do we find out?"

"You take a piece for yourself. Or you give me the girl and let me work."

"Give you the girl. For what?"

"Her blood, idiot." Alejandro looked at me like I was a cadaver for dissection in a science class. "Cade's a chivalrous fool. If he made her his solidaire in a bid to keep her safe, she'll have his blood in her veins, and it's a simple matter to lift it. If not, I'll cut her up trying various things, and then she's yours to do with what you wish. Leave her and the treasure with me. I'll have your answer in a few hours."

I wavered as I shook my head. "No."

That earned me a snort of laughter from Leith, a full chuckle from Brennan, and a headshake from the elfess.

Leith knelt to look at me. "Do you want to try paralysis again?"

I jerked away from him, falling against Alejandro's legs. Before I could get away, he'd caught me by the throat and pulled me upright against him, my back to his front. Rough fingers squeezed when I tried to protest again, cutting off my voice.

"You want this treasure free and clear?" Alejandro said. "Give me the girl and twelve hours. Oh, and a fifty percent cut when it's done."

Leith scowled. "Twenty percent and six hours."

"Thirty and eight," Alejandro countered.

"Fine. Done." Leith waved a hand. "Brennan, get the chest in there. Then get some zip strips on the halfling. I need to check in with the Captain. Nekane, with me."

With a last suspicious look, the elfess followed Leith to a side door as Brennan sighed, shut the lid, and hefted the chest.

I struggled as Alejandro marched me back to the room I'd been in, but prickles of magic swept over me.

"Don't," he murmured, almost too quiet for me to hear. "I have a proposition. You can listen, or I can pull your blood from your pores."

I stopped fighting, heart pounding, as we re-entered the room.

"Put the box there," Alejandro directed, pointing to the back of the room.

When Brennan passed him with a hateful glare and a wide berth, Alejandro shoved me aside, shut the door, and clubbed

Brennan in the back of the head with both hands in a knotted fist. When the elf dropped, he followed it up with a kick to the temple.

I had a minute to gape before Alejandro turned to me.

"Now," he said. "That proposition. I'll be fucked if I take any percent less than ninety-nine of this treasure. Lifting the curse will go faster if I don't have to fight you the whole way. Help me willingly, and I'll walk you out the front door myself."

"Out the front door where?" I rasped. I wasn't getting another shitty deal.

He sneered. "You're reasonably clever, I'll give you that. Fine. We'll walk out together. I'll go my way. You go yours. For now."

"Unharmed," I insisted.

"Unharmed beyond what I need to do to lift the curse."

I was making a deal with the devil, but I knew how unlikely it was I'd get out of here without help. There was no leaving completely unharmed. "What happens if you can't break the curse?"

Alejandro shrugged, eyes glittering. "Then I have my fun, and you're on your own. If I were you, I'd try to push Leith into killing me rather than stand trial. I hear the local queens have torture down to an art form."

"I want the gems."

He frowned at them, lips moving silently, then at me. "They're nothing special."

"Callista wanted all the gems. That's all of them. Give me those, and you have a deal."

"What the fuck does she want gems for?"

I shrugged and knelt as spent adrenaline sent me into a downward spiral, sparking defiance. "I don't know, and I don't care. Give me all the gems, or this deal is worthless to me and I will make this as long and as hard as I can."

The witch studied me, clearly fantasizing. "If we were in any other circumstances…" He groaned. "Such a tease. But done. The deal is made."

There had to be more questions I should ask, but time was of the essence. "The deal is made. What do you need from me?"

He pointed to the floor beside him. "Sit there. Don't speak. Don't move."

I did as he asked, praying this wasn't some elaborate trick.

But all he did was squint between me and the chest. "Get closer."

I shifted until my leg pressed against the cool wood, and it was only then I realized the lead in the cuff on my wrist was starting to leach through my pores and poison me. Sweat sheened on my skin, but I sat as still as I could while he circled, muttering to himself, before snagging his bag from near the door. Brennan groaned, and Alejandro casually kicked him in the head again before drawing an ornately carved blade and kneeling beside me.

"Don't move," he said as I tensed and started to shift away. "This is going to hurt like hell, and then it's going to burn in your veins. I'm going to say some words, you're going to repeat them while dripping your blood over the treasure. Understood?"

I nodded, gritted my teeth, and offered my left arm before he could grab it.

"Gods, what a woman." He sounded thoroughly aroused and looked even more so as he clasped my wrist and pulled it so my arm stretched over the box.

I hissed as he cut along my forearm and spoke three words slowly.

"Repeat them."

I did, although I had no idea what I was saying. It was the same language Cade had spoken to open the box, and as

Alejandro had promised, a new burn started rushing through me.

Another cut, another three words. Then a third cut and three more.

Blood dripped over the gold, and each series of words stretched the energy in the room tighter. Then, with a flick of the knife, he joined all three of the cuts with a shallower fourth one and spoke four more words.

I repeated them, my veins on fire, and the tension in the room fled as though cut with the knife.

"Haha!" Alejandro grinned. "So the old bastard did feed you. Lucky for both of us."

All I could do was waver. It felt like some of my vitality had been drawn into the spell, draining me as the magic lifted. When he released my wrist, I dragged my arm back toward me and clutched it close, trying to stem the bleeding as the burning sensation eased back down to the pain of lead poisoning.

It had worked. It had fucking worked, and I was a step closer to escape far faster than I'd dared to hope.

If Alejandro kept up his end of the deal. He'd lied once already, after all.

The witch dug in his bag and pressed a cloth into my hands. I wrapped it around my arm as he went back in and withdrew a small leather pouch, emptied it of some small bones, scooped all the now-bloodied gems into it, and dropped it into my lap before slamming the chest shut.

"Up, girl, up." He hefted the chest, making it clear I'd have to get up by myself. "Don't fail now, not with what this will cost you if you do." His grin had an edge to it. "However shall I hunt you down if you die here?"

Fighting off a wave of nausea at the very idea, I wobbled to my feet as he murmured a spell. Probably something to keep us hidden or our movement unheard.

One step. Another. And just as he had promised, we walked down the corridor and out the front door.

His red Altima was parked out front, and he shoved the chest in the passenger seat.

"I'd offer you a ride," he said, "but a deal's a deal. I suggest you start running."

With that, Alejandro turned his back on me and got in his car, not sparing me a backward glance.

"Fuck," I muttered.

Brennan would wake up sooner or later, or Leith would want for an update, or Nekane would be too smart not to check in. I jerked myself into a run or as close to one as I could manage, given I was exhausted, starving, dehydrated, bleeding, concussed, mildly lead poisoned, and whatever the fuck else had happened to me in the last twelve hours or however long it'd been. The uneven ground tried to trip me at every step, but if I could reach the main road, I might have a chance. Not much of one, given I was leaving a trail of footprints and probably blood, but anything was better than nothing.

Desperately, I made it down the slope the half-finished building was on. When it got steep, I sank to my ass and skidded down, caking my shorts with dirt and scraping the undersides of my bare legs, before struggling to my feet at the bottom. Not far. Alejandro made it to the main road and sped away, leaving me to my fate.

Go, Lya. Go. Keep moving.

Each step took me farther from the danger I knew and into dangers I couldn't see. In the early dark, I missed a dip in the land not far from the main road. I stumbled, at the end of my strength, and forced myself back up again. Exhaustion might kill me, but at least I'd save myself from Leith.

Only if I could get my body to move.

Another stumbling step and I crashed down, panting. A car was coming toward me. Something black.

My brain screamed at me. I had to hide. If it was a mundane, I couldn't let them call the police or an ambulance because I couldn't explain myself or the anomalies in my blood and DNA without breaking the Détente. If it was more elves, I definitely couldn't let them see me. Staying close to the ground seemed like a better idea, even if the construction site was likely littered with broken glass, stray nails, and other harmful debris.

I had to keep moving.

The car braked hard enough for the tires to screech and then reversed. I'd been spotted. I didn't waste breath cursing as I used the burst of adrenaline to push to my feet and lurch into a limping not-quite run.

Headlights flared as the car angled toward me. My breath heaved in so hard it hurt and out so hard I thought I'd never get it back. Then my feet went out from under me, and I tumbled into a drainage ditch. Stinking, muddy water splashed, and a cloud of mosquitoes hummed.

"Lya!"

I scrambled to my feet again at the stage-whispered shout. I couldn't stop now.

"Lydia, stop!"

It almost sounded like Cade, but he'd been abandoned on that dead-end road at the lake. He was dead.

Shouts rang out at the top of the hill, back at the construction site. The elves had discovered their prizes missing.

My foot slipped in the mud on the other bank, and I went down once more. A frustrated sob tore free. Something rattled in the grass next to my right hand, and I recoiled as I spotted the snake I'd almost fallen on.

The movement took me straight into the grasp of whoever was chasing me.

"Hekate damn it, stop running and come with me!"

Strong arms hoisted me up and over a shoulder. As I thumped against a muscled back, the waft of ash and iron with a hint of granite hit my nose.

"Cade?"

Chapter 20: Cade

Cade hadn't thought anything could top the fear Morris could instill in him, but spotting a haggard Lya, watching her drop into dirty water, and then getting her into the car, only to be powerless to help as she spasmed in pain next to him—that was far worse.

He didn't know how she'd gotten free, but it had to have been Fate turning a smile his way to find her fleeing a partially constructed building, the third one he'd tried in the area when the address Callista had given him had been empty. There were several office parks going up in this part of RTP, all in various stages of completion, some apparently more convenient than others for whatever the hell had been done to Lya for her to be terrified, covered in bruises, and smelling of fresh blood, not to mention passing out as soon as she was in the car.

The steering wheel creaked, and he forced his fists open and his thirst down. When he found who'd done this, hell wasn't going to be nearly enough to pay.

Lya stirred and groaned, panicking as she took in the unfamiliar car. Then her gaze fell on him. "Cade?"

"It's me. What do you need?"

"You're alive?"

"Of course, love. We're going somewhere safe."

"Nowhere's safe. Treasure's gone."

That broke his heart. Didn't she know he'd protect her? Although, he hadn't done a good job of it so far. He'd tried, but "backfired" was too small a word for what'd happened as a result. "Don't worry about it. We'll figure something out."

"Alejandro took it."

Cade frowned, wondering how the hell he'd tracked the treasure, but it didn't matter. The blood witch had had a plan all along, and if this one inconvenienced the elves, so much the better. "Okay, love. Rest now. We'll talk later."

She slumped back against the seat, a fine tremor rattling her entire body even when the road was smooth.

Driving as quickly as he dared given the heavy traffic on 40 and his own rusty skills, Cade navigated the borrowed car with his heart in his throat. Clouds swept in, and he prayed it didn't start to rain. He had no idea where the switch for the wipers was or how to turn them on. The whole way, guilt choked him, souring the hunger that'd risen at the scent of her blood. He'd been so focused on doing what he'd thought was best that he hadn't included her in any of it. Making connections hurt people, hurt *him*, but this time it wasn't him who was harmed. It was Lya.

He hadn't needed to become Morris, or even the shadow of his old self, to hurt someone. He'd done plenty simply by claiming her but not giving her the tools to protect herself.

The results were unacceptable.

Lya was still shaking when he pulled into the driveway of Terrence's duplex, and the sky chose that moment to open up with a downpour. The porch light came on, and the door leading to the other unit opened. Cade paused long enough to make sure it was Terrence and that he wasn't being ordered away before hurrying to Lya's side of the car, opening the door, and crouching.

"We're here, love. Can you walk to the door? I don't know how far the neighbors are."

"If I lean on you." Her chattering teeth broke up the words.

"Just put one foot in front of the other, and I'll take the weight, okay?"

She nodded jerkily, and he rose, pulling her upright and steadying her when she nearly went down. The arm he slipped around her waist touched bare skin, and she burned like she was feverish.

He swallowed his questions. He could figure out what was wrong once they were inside.

Terrence had unlocked the door and gone in ahead of them. The wereleopard laid out a first aid kit alongside a few small boxes with hand-scrawled labels and put a kettle on to boil. Anger snapped in his eyes as he looked Lya over. "Y'all can stay the night and the next day, gratis. I won't put one of us out, not when she's been beat all to hell like this for someone else's games."

"But I'm not one of you. I'm not a were," Lya slurred.

"I know that. You're still an Othersider, and in this house, we look after our own. Especially the ones who've been kicked." He nodded at Lya's speechlessness and clapped Cade on the shoulder as he passed. "I'll be back in an hour with some more meat. She looks like she's gonna need it."

"Thank you," Cade said. "Truly."

With a nod, Terrence left, locking the door behind him.

Lya wobbled, nearly going down, and Cade scooped her up.

"Why is he helping us?" she asked.

"Because he's a good person and we're in need."

She shook her head. "But I don't have the treasure anymore. I can't—"

"Don't worry about it. I paid for us and then some. Let's focus on cleaning you up, and we'll sort out Callista tomorrow, okay?"

Her lips pressed tightly shut, and a troubled look tightened her features. But she didn't argue as he set her carefully on the cracked tiles of the bathroom floor. She immediately pulled her knees up and wrapped her arms around them, teeth still chattering away.

Cade spotted the likely reason: a cuff pinching tightly around her left wrist and blood-spotted bandages wrapping the same arm. With gentle fingers, he took her hand. "Let's get this off."

He flexed it open, wincing at her gasp of pain. On examining the inside, he found not only a lead band, but also a small spike sticking out from the lead that matched a bleeding puncture in her wrist. The cruelty of it was enough to shock him out of the allure of her blood.

Forcing his tone to more gentleness than he felt, he asked, "Who put this on you?"

"Leith Sequoyah." She glanced at it and snarled. "That's not standard issue. That spike is custom. Fuck. I couldn't figure out why I was feeling so sick."

"Sequoyah." Again, Cade swallowed questions and observations about the elf he'd drunk from on Ocracoke. The Sequoyahs had a great deal to answer for. *Later. Focus on her now.*

She held out her arm and smiled wryly. "Help yourself. Glamour me a little first though. Please."

"You don't have to—"

"I want to. Close it up."

He leaned in to kiss her forehead before catching her eyes and easing her into a light glamour. The pained lines of her face and body eased as she slumped. Sealing his lips around the wound in her wrist, he pressed his tongue to it and locked his jaw to stop himself from biting her at the burst of herby flavor. When it was as healed as he could get it, he shifted his attention to her arm, hissing in outrage as he saw the four even cuts. "Who did this?"

Her lashes fluttered at his growl. "Alejandro. To break the curse."

More questions he couldn't ask even though fury burned in him. They'd had an agreement—Alejandro wasn't to touch her. But there was nothing to be done now except to do what he could to close up the evidence of that broken deal. Magic stung as he did, and he swallowed down a growl along with the taste of Lya.

The kettle whistled as he finished. "Are there any other open wounds?"

"No. Bruises, I think a sprain. Concussion."

"Okay. Can you wash up if I set you in the bath?"

She nodded, and he helped her out of her clothes before closing the shower curtain and turning it on. When the water was warm, he lifted her deadweight and put her in the tub. "Hang tight."

Back in the kitchen, he took the whistling kettle off the hob before checking the boxes Terrence had set out. Herbal teas, likely from the witches. One for sedation and nerves, a blood tonic, and the last for general vitality. He prepped the blood tonic, measuring out the prescribed amount of loose herb into the little metal tea ball and hurrying it to the bedroom to steep before heading back to the bathroom with the first aid kit.

"Lya? Need a hand?" he asked.

"Yeah."

Cade set the first aid kit on the counter, stripped out of his shirt, and helped her wash her back and hair. Once she was clean, he switched off the water, lifted her out, and dried her off before setting her on the toilet. Normally, she'd shout at him for babying her. That she wasn't now scared him almost as much as finding her had. She sat listless and still, like there was something more going on than being hurt and lightly glamoured, but she didn't say anything as he checked every inch of her, smoothing cream into bruises and bandaging partially healed cuts.

Words warred on his tongue, and he swallowed them all as guilt and shame burned in his chest. This had happened because he hadn't been strong enough to keep her and too slow to find her. If he'd just *listened* to her and stayed put, maybe—

Water splashed on his forearm, and he froze, looking up from the evaluation of her swelling ankle.

"I'm sorry," she said. Tears streaked her cheeks.

Shock stole any sensible reply. "What?"

"I'm sorry. You popped the solidaire question out of nowhere, and I didn't know what to do because I was so mad at you and so tired and I was scared about what it meant." She sniffled, and another tear dropped as words spilled out of her. "I thought you were laying in the road somewhere after I made that stupid turn and burning up in the sun and that you'd died thinking I hated you. But you still came—"

"Lya, no. Look at me."

She raised her eyes from her knees to his chest.

Cade tilted her chin up. "Eyes, my love."

They met his, flicked away, and came back, red-rimmed and damp with more tears.

"The only thing I have been thinking all day is what I would give to have you back, and what I would do to those who took you. Who hurt you. Understand?"

Lya nodded then reached for him. Cade eased her off the toilet and into his lap, squeezing her as tightly as he dared. She clung to him just as tightly and buried her face in his shoulder. He got a good grip on her legs and lifted her as he stood, carrying her to the bedroom. This was twice in a week that she'd cried in front of him, and he hated that he might be the cause of it. He knew better than to make any promises to her, but as he set her on the bed and propped her up against some pillows, he promised himself he'd do some serious soul-searching.

"Drink your tea, love," he said, holding it out to her.

She reached for it and pulled a face at the flavor but didn't argue. All this lack of argument worried the hell out of him. It wasn't like her, at all, and he hoped she was just tired and hurt.

Just tired and hurt.

The idea nearly made him snarl, but he didn't want her to think it was her fault. "I'm going to get you some water."

Lya nodded, still working on the tea with methodical sips.

When he came back, she'd set it aside and was studying the cuts in her arm.

"I want to do it," she said when he extended the glass to her. "I want to be your solidaire."

Cade wavered on his feet as emotion hit him—disbelief, love, desire so intense his heart skipped into a beat…and fear. He sank to the bed beside her and searched her face. "I—are you sure?"

"Yeah." She reached for his hand and pulled him closer when he gave it to her, continuing in a raspy voice. "Cade, the first thing I thought about when I woke up was you. Where you were. That you must have died. What you might have thought about me at the end."

"Don't do it for me. Do it because you see gains for yourself." Because he wouldn't be able to give her up, easily or at all, if she came to him like this, and he needed it to be her idea.

"I do. You said status and protection. I'm tired of having no status in Otherside. Like I'm some kind of honorary member. Goddess. A wereleopard who doesn't know me from Lilith offered me more respect than my own people ever did." Her eyes shone with tears that seemed equal parts pain, exhaustion, and anger. "I want more. I deserve more. If you want to give it to me, I'll take it." A smile flickered. "I love you too much to go anywhere anyway."

A knock on the front door interrupted before Cade could respond, and he was on his feet and in the doorway of the bedroom even as Terrence called out, "Coming in with Ximena, y'all decent?"

Cade glanced at Lya, and she shifted to get under the blankets.

"Decent enough," he said. "Be with you in a minute."

"I hope he has food," Lya whispered.

"I think he does. Stay here."

The weres were moving around in the kitchen when Cade walked in. Bulk food cartons were stacked on the counter, and Ximena was seasoning steaks while Terrence chopped vegetables.

Cade hesitated in the archway. "Can I help?"

"Nah, we got this," Terrence said.

"But you're two alphas. Surely, your people—"

Ximena snorted. "Will better learn service leadership and how to be a good community member when they see it demonstrated by their alphas. You're absolutely right."

The look she leveled at him warned him better than words to mind his own business.

Cade raised his hands. "We're much obliged."

"We know," Terrence said with a cat's smile. "But we have home training, even if the rest of Otherside doesn't. Go on and take care of your girl. We'll shout when dinner's ready."

"Thank you. For everything." Cade slipped out and returned to Lya. "Food will be ready soon."

"Thank the Goddess."

They stared at each other a few moments before she squirmed. "So, do I get the job?"

With a bark of laughter, he went to the suitcases he'd managed to keep and dug around in hers until he found a T-shirt and pajama shorts for her and a clean tee and jeans for him. It was maybe too casual to be guesting in, but he couldn't bring himself to care. They'd both been stretched to the limits of their endurance—Lya even more so than him, with less in reserve—and all he wanted for both of them was a night to breathe in safety and comfort.

When Lya had dressed and slipped lower under the covers, Cade took a quick shower and changed, gathering their dirty clothes to bring back with him.

She sat bolt upright when she spotted them, wincing and holding her head for a moment before saying, "The pockets. Check the pockets. Carefully."

Frowning, Cade did as she asked. His lips pressed together in a grim line when he found what was clearly an improvised lock pick in one, but in the other he found a bloody leather pouch. "What's this?"

"What Callista asked for. All the gems that remained."

He stared at her. "You were captive, bound, beaten, trapped into a deal with a blood witch, and still walked away with a pouch full of gems?"

A bemused look fell over her face. "When you put it that way…"

Shaking his head, Cade tucked it into his pocket and the clothes in a plastic bag in the suitcase, before retaking his place beside her on the edge of the bed and cupping her chin. "If you really meant it, about being my solidaire, I'm luckier than I ever knew to have found you."

Lya stared up at him with solemn, dark eyes. "I meant it. I want you. Forever."

Chapter 21: Lya

My heart pounded as Cade squinted at me. Was he having second thoughts? About my sincerity? I'd been flaky in the past when it came to commitment, but I meant it even though my heart pounded harder than my head and my mouth was dry from more than dehydration.

This was it.

I didn't know how I knew. I'd thought Henri was it, but I'd been wrong. I might be wrong again. But Henri had never come after me. He'd never done anything for me except make me come, and even there, Cade was better.

This was the right choice.

Cade was the right choice, my frustrating, adoring, protective vampire. He drove me insane sometimes, but I did the same to him. We still loved each other, no matter how mad we were. We always worked shit out and never let it get in the way of what mattered, this whole trip case in point. That was what mattered, wasn't it? He'd come for me, even though it meant going up against Callista and the Darkwatch. I could trust him, trust his intentions, even if he was kind of shitty at telling me things. We could work on that. I could have faith in him. In us.

"Cade?" I flushed at the waver in my voice. I really did want this, and I was afraid he'd change his mind.

Rather than answering, he shut the door then lay beside me, propped up on pillows against the headboard, and pulled me to him for a deep, lingering kiss. For a minute, I forgot all my aches and bruises. Forgot the looming danger of Callista as he claimed me with his lips, careful as ever with his fangs even as he deepened it.

"I am honored that you chose me," he murmured against my lips when I reluctantly pulled away for air. "If you're sure, you need to drink from me. It'll deepen the tie between us over time, and you'll heal quicker even now."

"I'm sure." I took a shuddering, anticipatory breath as he evaluated me again before biting hard into the top of his wrist then hovering it in front of my mouth. Without hesitating, I closed my mouth around it. The first swallow tasted exactly like blood smelled, but the second...

I didn't realize I'd gripped his arm until he was gently prying my fingers free. "Enough, love."

No. I needed more. It burned like strong liquor and hit my system like it. My head spun, my stomach clenched, my magic flared to life, and I didn't care. This was *good*, and it was *mine*.

"Lydia."

I opened my eyes and looked at him. His eyes were fully black, and a light glamour made me waver as he caught me in it. "Enough. You have forever and a day for more. Too much tonight will make you sick."

The glamour washed over me. I dropped back and released his arm. The wound started closing as soon as I stopped pulling on it, and he licked away the last smear.

The blood I'd drunk hit my system then, and I gasped, fisting my hands at the exquisite sensation that skated the knife's edge between pleasure and pain. I felt more awake and alive than I had in days, and some of the aches faded even as it seemed every nerve and muscle in my body was pulled tight. My eyelashes fluttered as I groaned, clutching him.

He watched me pant and writhe as the blood worked its way through my system, the darkness never leaving his eyes. "Easy, my love. Breathe." He pulled me closer and clasped my jaw, rubbing my cheek with a thumb. "It'll get less overwhelming with time."

Footsteps in the hallway preceded a knock at the door.

"Is she okay?" Terrence asked.

Cade pulled away enough to twist and speak over his shoulder. "She will be. Give us a few more minutes please."

"All right. Food'll be up in five."

"Thank you."

The burning finally subsided, and I slumped with a gasp as I was left with a renewed vitality and a sudden desire to fuck the daylights out of him. "That… Is it always like that?"

"Yes. A perk meant to keep our solidaires loyal, and the other reason it's not meant to be casually offered or a nightly thing once it is. Like I said, you'll learn how to manage it with time."

He'd fed me once before, but I'd been too out of it to remember. I could see why they rationed blood to their special someones only. If this was widely known, they'd be hunted. Chasing a glamour high was dangerous enough for both parties. This? This would be deadly.

"You want to bite me now," I said when I noticed his eyes were still black.

"I do, among other things. But you're healing and have given me too much lately. Next new moon though…" Pure hunger washed over his face, and he shuddered, closing his eyes in a long blink that did nothing to calm him. "If you're steady, go eat. I'll be there in a few minutes."

I pushed up carefully, surprised to find how much stronger I was already. Still aching, still bruised, but I felt like I'd had a few hours of sleep.

What would it be like after a year of this? Ten? Fifty? I grinned. I might have agreed to it out of love and self-preservation, but it felt damn good in more ways than one to know I'd benefit as well. I leaned in to kiss Cade's cheek then made my careful, limping way to the kitchen I vaguely remembered from when we'd arrived.

Our hosts were seated in the dining space on the other side of a bar window, already eating.

Terrence flicked a critical gaze over me then smiled. "There she is. Looking much better than you have a right to after the way he brought you in here."

"Cade takes care of me," I said before extending a hand to the woman. "Lydia, House Desmarais, solidaire to Cade." My heart fluttered to introduce myself that way, and I wrestled a silly smile down.

She put down her fork to shake it. "Ximena, jefa of the Jade Tooth jaguars. Be welcome in our home. Our table is yours, our hearth is yours, and our roof is yours, while you are here "

I inclined my head and offered the ritual response. "I honor my hosts. While your home is mine, my strength is yours." I grimaced. "Such as it is. I owe you both."

Terrence grinned as he shook my hand and then cut a slice of rare steak. "Your other half covered it, but I won't say no if you're looking to owe favors. Assuming Callista doesn't have your head over whatever all this is about. Now sit and eat something before you fall."

I did as he said and served myself. The steaks were huge— exactly what I needed to recover—and seasoned so well I groaned in pleasure. "Goddess, this is good."

"Been a rough few days for you?" Ximena asked.

I nodded. "Understatement."

Cade ghosted into the room, moving a little slower than usual, and settled into the chair next to me and across from

Terrence. His pupils were still a little too wide, but at least they'd pulled back in from his sclera.

Ximena gave him a wary look before deciding he wasn't going to bite anyone. "I assume y'all have a plan for tomorrow?"

Glancing at me, Cade said, "I was thinking tonight. I don't want to put any of us in more danger, given your generosity, and the sooner Callista gets what she asked for, the better."

Terrence made a cat-like *whuff* that sounded equal parts amused and derisive. "I reckon you ain't giving her all she's got coming, but—"

"Terrence," Ximena snapped.

He grinned, even in the face of her cat's red-gold eyes staring him down, and shook his head. "All I'm saying is, sooner she gets whatever it is she wants, the sooner she might turn her attention back to justice."

"Hear, hear." I toasted them with my glass of water and drank, pissed all over again at how I'd been treated in pursuit of Goddess only knew what ambition.

"See?" Terrence grinned and looked back at Cade. "So. You'll see the Arbiter tonight, sleep the day and…"

"Leave in the evening," Cade said firmly. "With my sincere thanks for the additional day."

I nodded. "Yes. Thank you." My relief melted as I remembered a key detail. "My car—"

"Is in our shop," Ximena said. "Repairs'll be done tomorrow. Damage was mostly to the side panel, mirror, front bumper, headlights, and tires, but we'll test the steering column and powertrain as well."

"Thank you." I smiled then frowned at my empty plate when my fork scraped. I'd cleaned the plate.

Terrence gestured for me to serve myself from a platter of steak, another of potatoes, and a bowl of spinach, pea, and bean salad. Slightly embarrassed for my higher-than-normal appetite,

I served myself. Cade just nodded, as though that was to be expected.

When I started working on my second plate, he said, "If you'll all excuse me, I'll go take care of that business now."

"Wait," I said when he started to rise. "I want to go with you."

"Lya—"

"I know you just got me back. But she assigned the job to me. I need to finish it."

Frustration snapped in his dark eyes, and he pressed his lips together the way he did when he really wanted to say something that was almost guaranteed to piss me off. Then he sighed, leaned over, and kissed my forehead before sitting all the way back down. "As you wish."

I didn't miss the look the cats exchanged, but they didn't say anything.

Terrence changed the subject to ridiculing the latest werewolves-versus-vampires movie, lightening the mood with snarky observations of what they'd gotten wrong from both an Othersider and a military tactics standpoint.

It felt good, being in community like this. Feeling like I belonged somewhere, even if everyone around this table was a different faction or sub-faction. The guilt I'd felt at committing treason smoothed a little—still there, still jagged, but easier to carry. The elves might technically be my people, but the werecats were risking what little they had compared to the other factions in town to help me.

And Cade had made an irrefutable place for me among the vampires. Yeah, we were all different, but we were united in that we were all struggling for a fair place in Otherside.

For once, I felt like I'd found my people.

When we finished dinner, I went and changed while Cade cleared the table and loaded the dishes into the dishwasher.

Terrence and Ximena were gone when I got back, and I sank into a chair to wait for Cade to finish when he waved me off.

"Alejandro owes me a machete, and the Darkwatch owes me a knife," I complained. The one I'd had strapped to my forearm when I was taken was gone, but Cade had gotten everything else.

"Better they owe you a knife than me a solidaire." The words were soft, but silken danger laced through them.

I started to make him promise he wouldn't do anything then swallowed it.

He turned to me in surprise. "You're not going to warn me off them?"

Shrugging, I shook my head. "They have it coming. I wouldn't have had to commit treason if everyone here hadn't put me in a fucking impossible situation."

Cade loaded the last dish, washed his hands, and stalked over to me as he dried them, somehow managing to look threatening even with mussed-up hair and a dishcloth patterned with yellow flowers.

"Good." He leaned on the table and lowered his face to mine. "Because if *anyone* tries to take you from me again, there *will* be hell to pay."

I swallowed hard at the brief flare of his pupils into deadly black then tilted my head. His lips crashed down on mine with a passion I wished we could take straight to bed, even if I wouldn't be able to do much more than lay there. I swiped my tongue over one of his fangs, enjoying the way he groaned, gripped my arms, and pulled me upright.

Stupid to tease the vampire, but I'd never get tired of being wanted like this.

He pulled himself away and gripped my chin with firm fingers. "You are the naughtiest little—"

I stole another kiss to shut him up and grinned. "I know. Let's get going. Sooner we get there, sooner we can go to bed. I'm knackered. And I missed you."

With a growl, he took a deep inhale and patted the pocket with the gems. "Sounds like a plan."

I lost a little of my courage on the way over and whipped it into mental bravado instead. I'd survived when I suspected I wasn't supposed to, and I would see this through. To distract myself, I asked, "How did you find me, anyway?"

His hands tightened on the wheel. "I made a deal with Callista."

"You what? That's exactly what—"

"I know. But I needed to get you back."

"What did you agree to?"

Cade smirked. "I told her it was a custom spell that could only be broken by blood from Morris's line."

Confused, I said slowly, "But Alejandro broke it with mine. I mean, I had to repeat some words but it didn't seem that hard. Definitely nowhere near the eight hours he bargained for."

"That's because I lied. Morris's line was true, but the rest? Morris was a cheap bastard who'd rather hoard wealth than spend it. He had the money to buy something custom, and he had enough paranoia that I'm surprised he didn't. But any blood witch would have been able to break it with an idea of the language used and one of us as a willing participant." He glanced at me and sobered. "I guess that's the one good thing about you being as drained as you were in June. I don't think the virus would have sunk in enough for you to count as being of the bloodline otherwise."

"Silver linings," I murmured as I reached over to squeeze his thigh.

We pulled into the dirt lot in front of Callista's bar, and I took a deep breath. Then another and a third, as I psyched myself up.

Cade just sank into the thunderous mood he got when someone was about to have a bad day.

"Let's go." I slipped out of the car, clutching my purse to me, and followed him inside.

Chapter 22: Lya

Callista looked up from the bar, her eyes narrowing as they fell on us, and a trio of elves at one table stared icily at me.

Shit. Word's gotten out.

Tonight was make-or-break in too many ways, and my heart jumped into my throat as a cold sweat broke out over me. Suddenly I was wondering if it would have been wiser to stay at Terrence's and rest.

But I was here, so we were doing this.

When we were close enough to the bar for Callista to speak in a whisper, she sneered at us. "I wasn't expecting to see either of you again. Either you'd be dead, or you'd have more sense to show your faces here."

Wordlessly, Cade dug in his pocket and slapped the blood-stained pouch on the bar counter before speaking in the same ugly tone she had. "I take it you don't want this then?"

The sudden blankness of her expression said as much as a shout would have. "What is that?"

"What you asked for," I said.

She glared between us then jerked her head toward the door to the back. We followed, and I did my best to ignore the elves. I was beyond their reach now. I hoped.

As soon as the door was closed behind the three of us, Callista held out her hand imperiously. "Give it to me."

Cade clenched it in his fist. "Lya is mine, as solidaire. The elves can't have her. I don't give a fuck what deal you made with them for the treasure."

"So long as you have my gems, then fine, the little bitch is yours."

I stiffened, seeing as this little bitch was standing right here, but kept my mouth shut. This was Cade's bargain now.

He didn't hand over the pouch. "She's *all* mine, Callista—body, blood, and soul. Free and clear of all debts, obligations, indentures, deals, and the terms of her exile."

It grated to be bargained over like a thing, but the terms of my exile were ironclad. House Monteague had agreed to what Desmarais had offered, but as Arbiter, Callista had the final word and, more importantly, the power to enforce it.

She scowled. "Show me the gems first."

"No. You agree to this now or we walk with them." He shifted his fingers to make the stones grind together. "Lya, what's in here?"

I thought fast, knowing that what Callista sought probably wasn't it. "All of the gems that were in the chest when I escaped." It was a fine line to add "when I escaped." Fully the truth and yet not all the gems that'd been in the chest to begin with.

Her green eyes sparked with a murderous glare. "Everything in the chest?"

"Every gem that was in there when I was able to get my hands on it, yes."

"And how exactly did you manage that?" She smiled at Cade, sickly sweet. "Your lover seems to think you were kidnapped and being held, but you two have played a fast game before, I know you have. Tell me the truth."

I glanced at Cade, and he nodded infinitesimally. "The elves had a blood witch."

"What?" If I'd thought she was pissed before, she was furious now. "Where the fuck—"

"I think he was following us." Before she could get specific with her question, I raised the arm Alejandro had cut. "He beat the shit out of Brennan Sequoyah and threatened me into helping him. He seemed to think I could do something about the spell. I told him I'd try if I could have all the gems."

"And this blood witch just agreed?" she said disbelievingly.

I nodded and tried to work spit back into my mouth. Callista never got less terrifying, and my earlier high was crashing fast. "There was a whole Goddess-burning chest of treasure, and gold is easier to melt down and sell than gems, I don't bloody know. He agreed, fucked up my arm, made me say some shit. I guess it worked because…"

I trailed off and looked pointedly at the leather pouch still in Cade's grip.

Callista's eyes narrowed, and magic prickled over me. "Show me. In your hand."

Cade steadied my hands when I cupped them and dumped the whole bag in. A wealth of perfectly cut beauty winked under the light, rubies and sapphires, a few diamonds in various colors, opals, and the biggest black pearl I'd ever seen.

After a tense few seconds, Callista grunted. "So she really is your solidaire."

"I told you she was," Cade growled. "Satisfied?"

She hovered her hand over the gems piled in mine, and I held my breath as magic prickled again. "It's not there. What did you do with it?"

"Nothing!" I couldn't keep the note of fear out of my voice at the betrayal and rage in hers. "I took exactly what was there, all of it. If you don't find what you expected, ask the elves or the blood witch. The chest was open. We opened it just to make sure there were even gems inside after we got it and then came back here."

But not straight back, and I prayed she thought the waver was just fear and not guilt that apparently the djinn had been right about which gems Callista would want.

"Callista…" Cade's tone was flat and promised just as much violence as her expression and the increasingly sharp pricks of magic. "You heard what happened. I didn't know the full details of what was in the chest originally. If you didn't either, this is not on Lya. She had nothing to go on, was attacked by sirens and elves, cut up by a damned blood witch, and still managed to get what you'd asked for. Remember that we don't always get what we want, take what she's brought as a tax, and turn her over to me."

Half-truths on top of half-truths. Cade might not have known the full or original contents, but we both knew a soul gem or two had been in there. If we got out of this, it'd be by the smallest breath between the truth and a lie and his claim on me.

"Which elves?" she said in a whisper.

My hands were shaking more now, and I held them steady by sheer force of will. "Brennan Sequoyah was at the beach. Leith Sequoyah led the team that took me. He had the chest while I was unconscious."

Another act of treason piled on top of the rest, throwing elves under the bus to avoid damning Cade and me by telling her about the djinn. I was too tired and angry to care. I was done protecting the people who abused me at every turn for being what I'd been born as. Leith and the Sequoyahs in particular had it coming.

"And the witch?"

Cade snarled. "The Marqués Alejandro Alfonso Olivares de Guzmán, most recently of Florida."

"An old name," Callista said.

"An old acquaintance and an older witch. I imagine he was watching me for some time before coming up with a plan."

Callista nodded, looking as though she was marking each name down in her mind. "You have plenty of enemies still living, Cade. See that you don't get your new pet killed, hm?" She held out her hands, and I carefully poured the gems into them and wiped my hands on my jeans. "Don't even think about asking for your ten percent."

I shook my head, knowing better, even if I really could have used one of those.

Carelessly, she dumped all the stones on her desk like they were worthless and returned her attention to us, her ire shifting to thoughtfulness as she looked between us. "I find myself in the vexing position of having a bare hint of respect for the two of you. It's fairly obvious you colluded over Morris, even if I don't have enough proof of my own to call Maria a liar. Now you defy my orders, evade the Darkwatch, and survive a siren."

"Three," I whispered, shuddering. "There were three of them. A fourth came with the chest."

Her eyebrows lifted. "So you weren't exaggerating when I asked about your resume."

I shrugged, decidedly uncomfortable with where this might be going and feeling weaker by the second. We needed to leave before I crashed right here in her office.

"I could use people like you on my payroll," Callista finally said. "If you don't want to be Watchers, I'm sure I'll have need of bounty hunters sooner or later, especially lacking the gem I sought. Agree to come when I call, and I'll rescind your banishment and smooth things over with Torsten. Stay in the state or go, I don't care, as long as I can rely on you."

Cade and I looked at each other. He tilted his head so slightly I almost missed it. It was my decision.

I wanted to tell her to go fuck herself. But my car was still being repaired, I needed rest to heal, and I had a feeling that if we didn't agree, we weren't going to be given time for either. She might be presenting this as a choice, but we didn't have the power in this situation. There was no choice, not if we wanted to go free tonight, and she knew it. I nodded, nearly as imperceptible in my movement as he'd been.

Cade inclined his head to Callista. "We accept."

"Excellent." She waved a hand. "Now get the fuck out of my bar and stay out of trouble for at least a week."

I offered the same incline of my head and hustled out. Cade followed, and when he shut the door behind him, he offered me his arm. I took it, grateful for the support, and we left together. I kept my head high and didn't look at anyone on the way out.

Silence reigned the whole way home, both of us lost in thought and me too tired to find something to say. Cade was agitated, or as agitated as he allowed himself to get, tense and tapping a single finger on the steering wheel.

He'd tell me eventually. He was the brooder; I was the runner.

I dragged myself up the stairs when we got to Terrence's place, nodding when the wereleopard poked his head out, lifted his eyebrows, and grinned.

"So you survived," he drawled. "Good for you. Y'all get some rest." He glanced into the huge oak in the yard, and I followed his line of sight to spot a pair of eyes glowing in the dark from the lower branches. A sentry.

"Thank you, for everything. We'll be out of your hair tomorrow," I said.

He saluted and went back inside.

I let Cade steer me into our side of the duplex. By now, I was using the wall to support myself, still better than I had been when Cade had found me but far from a hundred percent and with the last few days catching up hard.

"Go to bed," he murmured. "I'll join you in a few minutes."

I just nodded and made my slow way there. I couldn't be bothered to put clothes back on again after stripping out of the ones I'd worn to see Callista, so I dropped into the bed, grateful for the soft mattress and softer sheets. They had a faint werecat scent of musk and cedar, but it wasn't unpleasant. Hell, right now it signaled safety. I curled up on my side and tried to figure out why I felt like I was about to cry.

I'd been doing too much of that lately, and I didn't like it. I was stronger than that. I dealt with shit with action, not with tears, but I just kept—

I sniffled. Something wasn't right. I couldn't figure out what it was. I should be happy. I'd gotten my freedom. I'd tied myself to a man I loved, one who would do anything for me, and gained standing for myself in Otherside. So what the fuck was wrong? I tried reaching for anger instead, but exhaustion smothered it.

The hall light went out, leaving the room dark except for the moonlight, and the mattress dipped as Cade slipped into bed behind me.

"Lya?" he said.

I swallowed past the lump in my throat. "Yeah?"

"What's wrong?"

"I don't know." The truth burst out before I could think about it, and that nearly broke the dam I was using to hold everything in.

He eased closer, pulling me into him by careful degrees before propping his head on his hand and resting the other arm lightly around my waist. "I need you to know something."

I squirmed, already uncomfortable for a reason my gut anticipated but my mind couldn't or wouldn't see. "What?"

"I spoke about you to Callista the way I did because that's what she expects from a vampire, especially one my age. That we think we own the people in our proximity and that their lives are simply another thing to claim, collect, and trade over our long courses of existence."

I flinched as his words pried loose the chip I hadn't realized was holding me down.

"I don't own you, love. I never could, as much as I might try. You're a wildfire, and I know that to try to control you would smother you until you went out or flared up to immolate me. You're free to burn however you please, and that includes blazing a trail away from me."

That was it. That was what had been bothering me.

It'd annoyed me in Callista's office, but I hadn't realized how much it'd sunk claws into me, made me feel like a thing rather than a person until he said it. I turned over, reading his expression, and found only solemnity.

Cade shifted his hand to my hip and rubbed slow circles with his thumb. "I know what it is to be owned and powerless and broken by it. I might overstep trying to protect you, and I might get frustrated when you don't want or need me to. But the ties that bind us are yours to strengthen or to break." A wry smile twisted his lips. "It's not quite the way a solidaire relationship typically works, but I'd rather adapt and entice you to stay than try to press my will and force you."

I couldn't find words, so I used actions, pressing myself tightly against him and kissing him deeply. This was why I trusted him. This was why I loved him. He *saw* me, saw into me and my heart and my needs in a way that nobody else had ever even bothered to try.

"I love you," I murmured against his mouth. "And I'm not going anywhere anytime soon."

I fell asleep in his arms, feeling respected and wanted. Loved.

Epilogue: Cade

"Cade?"

Lya's shout and the front door closing pulled his head up from the stack of papers she'd left for him to sign. Mind-numbing stuff, but between her modern knowledge and her sometimes peculiar way of seeing things, she was finding all manner of ways to diversify their income.

Like this latest endeavor. Inspired by the werecats' generosity, she'd talked him into investing in properties around St. Augustine which could be short-let to mundanes as vacation rentals but allocated to Othersiders in need of refuge otherwise. It was almost enough to make him wish he'd taken a solidaire earlier, except that would have meant he wouldn't have been able to take her on.

Soft footsteps pulled him out of his thoughts.

"You up, babe? Oh, there you are." She glanced at the tidy stack of papers and grinned, knowing how much modern contracts bemused him with their terms and conditions and the tiny print they were all written in. "All good?"

"Quite," he said. "Come here."

Rather than bristling at his commanding tone, she shook her head, and her smile widened as she hid something behind her back. He studied her, subtly scenting the air and trying to read her mood. Late autumn had brought out a new side of her, one that was more playful and less fearful. He wasn't sure if it was settling into their new life or her finding her stride with their relationship, but it looked good on her. The slight defensive hunch had eased from her shoulders, and she was more open to letting him take care of her. Maybe she simply understood how invested he was in doing so now.

"What have you got planned?" he asked.

"Guess."

"Love, I haven't the slightest idea what—"

"What day is it?"

Cade frowned, having fallen out of the habit of paying daily attention to the date centuries ago, unless there was something he was supposed to be doing. "Umm…"

Scoffing, she rolled her eyes and rushed him. Only his vampiric reflexes had him turning his chair to her in time to catch her as she dropped onto his lap, still hiding something behind her back.

"You seriously don't know?" she asked.

Glancing at the papers where he'd left the date blank because he seriously didn't and didn't want to break his focus to fetch his phone and check, he shook his head.

"It's your birthday!" She hesitated. "Right? November first? Or is that something you made up?"

"Oh, that. Yes, that's it. All Saints' Day." The irony of his damned self being born on a holy day never escaped him. He'd changed the year on his papers over the centuries and occasionally his name, but he'd always kept his original birthday. Something to tie him to who he'd been, even as he left that man in an unmarked grave.

Her smile lit up her face again, and she kissed him. "Good. Because I have a present for you."

Bemused and more than a little flattered that she'd bothered, he leaned back in his chair and rested his hands on her thighs. "Do you now?"

Lya nodded then hesitated again, suddenly uncertain. "I— If you don't like it, tell me, okay? I won't be upset."

"Well, now I have to know."

Shyly, she pulled her hands from behind her back. A small box was in each, and the way she squirmed on his lap made him wish he'd gone hunting before sitting down to paperwork.

She lifted one closer to him. "That's yours."

He took it with an amused smile. "Did you buy yourself a present for my birthday?"

"Yes, but it's the other half of your present."

Beyond curious, Cade opened the box to find a ring made of braided strands of red and gold metal. His finger tingled as he brushed it, entranced by its delicate strength. Before he could ask its meaning, she popped open the other box to show him a second, done smaller.

"They're spelled," she explained. "By the witch we helped last month. Bronze to link us. Copper to boost it. Gold for love. So if we get separated again, it's easier to find each other." She glanced down, squirmed again, and back up. "And as a symbol of commitment. If you like it…if it's okay…we each put a drop of blood on each ring to activate them and another drop each year to renew it."

Cade stared at her, feeling fit to burst. She'd done this? For him? For *them*?

"If you don't like it—"

He set the box on the table and shifted his hands to her hips to pull her flush against him then caught the back of her head to capture her mouth with a kiss.

"Is that a yes then?" Some of her confidence was returning.

"That's a yes." He rested his forehead against hers. "For you, it's always a yes." That she was doing this told him she might still run sometimes, but she was giving him a way to find her. A tie that said needing space wasn't abandonment. Connection didn't have to hurt, and he'd do anything to make sure she knew she was loved and cherished despite what others had done to make her fear she couldn't be—even if it meant rewriting what it meant to be master and solidaire.

Lya made an excited little noise at his acceptance, and he let her go when she bounced up. Setting the rings side by side on the table, she fetched her purse and pulled out another box, this one longer and slimmer, grinning at him.

"What's that?" he asked.

The ornately carved steel knife revealed when she opened it took his breath away. It was too small and thin to be useful for anything practical.

Except maybe ceremonial bloodletting. Hunger roared up in him as she presented it to him.

Cade plucked it out, admiring it before looking at her. She was flushed with anticipation and starting to smell way too fucking good in her excitement.

"Is this what I think it is?" he asked.

She nodded. "I didn't want to use a kitchen knife for the rings. I wanted it to be special." A sly smile made his heart beat. "But maybe we could use it for other things."

"You are the worst tease." Ideas flickered through his mind, and he pushed them down. It'd be another couple of weeks before they could enact them, longer maybe before he could suss out how she'd feel about some of his ideas, and he'd drive himself mad if he let his mind wander now.

Lya extended her left pinky finger to him. "Mercury finger. For communication. Sympathetic magic, I guess."

Gently, he clasped her hand and pressed the point of the knife to the extended finger. The keen edge drew blood immediately, and she smeared a little on each ring. Then he handed the knife over for her to prick his finger, and he did the same. A small pulse of magic sent tingles over them both, and she grinned when the blood soaked into both and was gone.

"All done," she said.

Cade caught her hand again, keeping his gaze on hers as he slipped it over her left pinky finger. She did the same for him, suddenly solemn, and they both gasped as a faint awareness of the other settled over them.

"Stay here," she said, heading for the door. "I want to see how it works. And you, get something to drink!" she called over her shoulder.

He did as she said, willing to break into his emergency cache of blood for whatever else she had planned for the evening. He got the sense of her running around the house, occasionally changing direction and moving closer to the front gate before returning, then running down the road. It would take some getting used to, but he'd rather have it than not, remembering how frantic he'd been to find her when her kin had taken her.

By the time she came back inside, he'd warmed and mostly finished his bag of AB positive. Lya approached at a slow, stalking pace, bringing the scent of outside air and her own perspiration closer.

"Don't get up," she said when he finished the blood and started to rise. "You're the birthday boy, and I'm here to serve."

She knelt between his knees and undid his jeans, pulling them down when he lifted up. He couldn't help tangling his fingers in her hair as she dragged her nails along the insides of his thighs then kissed her way from his knees to his groin. When she took his balls into her mouth and smoothed her tongue over them, he let his head fall back as he groaned.

"Fuck, Lya."

She hummed, pulling another groan from him, and kept teasing him until the blood he'd drunk made its way south to give him a throbbing erection. Then the heat of her mouth enveloped him, her throat working to take all of him. He kept her there when she managed it, unable to help himself from taking this small bit of control. When her hands tightened on his thighs, he released her, allowing her to fall back with a gasp before directing her motion again. Her lips slid along his shaft, tongue swirling, until all he could focus on was the cresting pleasure and his balls tightening and—

Cade grunted as he spilled his seed down her throat. When she'd drained him, he released her and slumped in the chair, unable to deny his secret enjoyment of seeing her like this: his, claimed and wanting with bright eyes and flushed face, the life in her so close to the surface with her pounding heart and heavy breath.

After centuries of being too afraid to love, he'd be damned if he let anyone come between him and this incredible woman—and the next person who tried would be deader than he was.

Want more?

This is the second book in a spin-off series, and there's plenty more to the world of Otherside.

You can get more Shadows of Otherside content in a few different ways:
- Read the original series
  - On Amazon: whwrites.com/soo-series
  - Elsewhere: whwrites.com/books
- Subscribe to Whitney's Patreon for bonus chapters from multiple points of view: whwrites.com/patreon
- Join Whitney on social media:
  - Twitter: twitter.com/write_wherever
  - Instagram: instagram.com/write_wherever
  - Facebook: facebook.com/WhitneyHillWrites

Sign up to the Write Wherever newsletter for updates: whwrites.com/newsletter.

Lastly, if you enjoyed this book, **please consider posting a review**, recommending it on Goodreads or BookBub, or telling a friend who might also enjoy it. As always, thank you for reading, and for your support!

Acknowledgments

No matter how many books I publish, that feeling of "omg I hope readers like it" never goes away. So thank you to all the enthusiastic readers who let me know how much they enjoyed Lya and Cade's first story.

Thanks and shout-outs to my family: Mom, Dad, Seester, and the extended family members who are just the best bedrock of support any author could hope for. My mom gets an extra special shout-out this time, because of something she said to me a few years ago at the NCMA when I was embarrassed about publishing smutty writing. Thanks, Mom. I hold that in my heart and it gives me courage when I start to worry about what people might think.

In that vein, RSL gets a special shout-out as well, for continually asking me, "But what if it *does* work out?" when I'm doom-spiraling about all the things that could go wrong.

I'm forever grateful to Jeni Chappelle for guiding me through yet another book and helping me keep my head on straight. What a fantastic partner to have in the writing and editing process!

My Patreon supporters get a massive thank you as well. Your enthusiasm for the universe of Otherside is part of what keeps me writing it.

To my beta and ARC readers, thank you for making my work better and shouting it from the rooftops. You're amazing!

And last but not least, thank you to every single reader who has taken a chance on a Black indie author and in so doing, taken my books into your homes, ereaders, and hearts.

Thank you all.

Also by Whitney Hill

About the Author

Whitney Hill is an author and speaker. The bestselling first book in her Shadows of Otherside series, *Elemental,* was the grand prize winner of the 8th Annual Writer's Digest Self-Published E-Book Awards and a Finalist in the Next Generation Indie Book Awards. Her second book, *Eldritch Sparks,* was named one of the Top 100 Indie Books of 2021 by *Kirkus Reviews.*

When she's not writing, Whitney enjoys hiking in North Carolina's beautiful state parks and playing video games.

Learn more or get in touch: whitneyhillwrites.com
More books by Whitney: whitneyhillwrites.com/original-fiction
Sign up to receive email updates: whwrites.com/newsletter

Join her on social media:
- Twitter: twitter.com/write_wherever
- Instagram: instagram.com/write_wherever
- Facebook: facebook.com/WhitneyHillWrites

Get bonus content on Patreon: patreon.com/writewherever